THE CŒUR D'OR MYSTERY

by

Anthony Day

Published by Columbine Pictures Press
Copyright © 2018 Anthony Day and Columbine Pictures Press

ISBN: **0995555680**
ISBN-13: **978-0995555686**

The Cœur D'or Mystery is the second in a series of comic novellas chronicling the adventures of two fiery yet elegant flappers; Samantha Bishop and her companion Nicola White.

PROLOGUE

*

It's the second and final lap of the Mille Miglia. In the lead are France's Pierre Gilbert and Jean Ginsburg. Second are Germany's Heinz Bahn and Franz De Burke.

*

And after a fine Cote du Rhone with a little light lunch, bringing up third is that plucky little pair of English lovelies, showing just how the fairer sex is a match for their men-folk, Miss Samantha Bishop and Miss Nicola White.

*

Hope they haven't smudged their lip-gloss! Aren't they the darling duo? You won't see many grease monkey's wearing that shade of red lip-gloss. Well, not outside of Brighton at any rate!

*

ANTHONY DAY

1

The winding, narrow, mountain road twisted and turned, tightly hugging the sheer, almost polished, slippery grey-blue rocks that jutted precariously out from the straight sides and into the dusty, dry road.

The three racing cars were tearing along, their over-large, wire wheels kicking up the dust, the throaty roar of the straight-eight engines echoing through the crisp, clear air from under their long bonnets.

Sitting behind the large wheel of the dark-green Riley nine, the fiery wildcat Samantha Bishop peered out through grey, dust-and-dirt stained glass of her goggles, fighting hard to hold the car in line, her white racing overalls and matching leather helmet also stained with the dirt and dust of the race. The front constantly weaved with the road as they bounced over potholes and rocks while she steered though the cloudy blue haze kicked up from the blue and the silver cars ahead of them.

She was in her element. She could feel the adrenaline coursing through her veins, pumping her heart quickly, almost as quickly as the car itself, but her hands were steady as her eyes watched the two cars ahead of her.

Not since she raced at Brooklands after she had left her French school and returned to England had she felt so alive and not since she had been an actress in the United States had she felt so determined to prove herself to other people. It wasn't going to be easy as both the drivers ahead of her were two of the best in all of Europe, and also her friends, as she had come to know them both well over the years, watching them race in the Men's events after her own were finished.

Beside Samantha sat her navigator, dressed the same, but reading a red, leather-bound notepad and holding the map on her lap, her companion and teammate, Nicola White. She was a couple of years younger than Samantha, being still only in her teens, and wasn't so comfortable with the speed they were travelling at. She also wasn't too happy with the height they were reaching either, closing her eyes every time the little Riley Nine's wheels drifted to the very edge of the cliff road so she wouldn't have to see the sheer drop and the tiny houses, the size of a hen's egg, below.

Suddenly they rode a bump and Nicola was knocked into the side of the car and for a moment she lost her place on the map as she slid back across the seat, thumping into Samantha. Not that she really needed the map here in the mountains. In the valley, through the streets, her map-reading skills were important, but here, where there was only the one road and one way, well, one way if you wanted to stay on the road, knowing where she was on the map, Nicola felt, would only help her to know where she was about to die.

Since leaving her home in Newcastle and travelling down to London, she had known some great times with

Samantha. She'd been to bars and clubs as well as theatre plays and the pictures and now the adventure included racing around Italy at the invitation of Samantha's oldest friend Porky.

It has started with a telegram a month before, and a few days after it had arrived, he'd come round to discuss taking part in the race. Several bottles of red wine, a decanter of whiskey and a dozen cigars later, he'd convinced Samantha to drive as he'd had the notion to put a team into this race this year and had thought of her as he knew in her heart she really wanted to get back into racing and she'd agreed, though she had made it a condition that Nicola would be her navigator.

So here they were, while Porky was enjoying himself in Rome drinking and talking about his chances in the race, Samantha was actually doing the racing, and doing well, third and still half a lap to go.

Porky was the son of some Lord. She couldn't remember which one as there were so many people in society to remember, and being with Samantha it had all been a whirl. She had found, in meeting them, most of the time they were best forgotten, but he was her best friend. He had met Samantha in her earlier racing days, before the pictures took her away from all that, and had easily known how to persuade her this would be a swell, jolly jape. And as promised, it was all the bees' knees. It was all such a heady, overwhelming ride she just wished would never end.

Nicola wiped a piece of dust from her goggles and looked at the silver Mercedes and blue Bugatti ahead of them.

All three were close, the two in front nose to tail, almost touching, as they jostled and weaved from side to side, one trying to pass, the other blocking, and, as they jousted with each other, the little Riley closed, until it almost shunted the rear of the Mercedes and had to quickly drop back. Each time she saw a gap almost big enough to dart though, Samantha tried, but each time being forced back by the winding, twisting turns of the mountainous road.

The other two cars were left-hand drive, but even though it meant she was closer to the mountain slope and could almost smell the blossom of the small white, pink and blue flowers sprouting between the joints of the rocks, not being able to see the drop, Samantha felt she was being too cautions, not willing to go too close to the edge in case she made a mistake, her only clue each time was how Nicola would flinch as she came close, but knowing how nervous her companion was, she suspected there were really feet to spare.

Samantha pushed the pedal to the floor, the pistons surged and the long bonnet of the car lurched. She could feel the hungry energy inside, unleashed, pull them effortlessly over the slippery gravel road, stones and chips of rock in the dust as it kicked out from the deep grooves of the tyres, rattling against the large wings as quickly, with effortless ease, their car caught up again with the other two cars, almost touching the rear of the silver Mercedes.

She let off a little on the accelerator pedal and pulled gently on the huge steering wheel as she tried to slide the car inside the Mercedes but the driver, seeing her in his wing mirror, pulled over slightly, narrowing the gap, so that she had to ease off again and fall back a foot or two behind him.

Still fighting the wheel, she glanced over to Nicola, who was looking down at her map and, suddenly aware she was being looked at, turned to Samantha as a warm smile crept across her lips.

As the three racing cars closed, a drystone wall on the cliff edge began to wiggle in towards the mountain as they came through a narrow section. Quickly, they filed behind one another, the Bugatti, followed by the Mercedes and then the Riley. Almost touching bumper to bumper, between the stone wall and the mountain side, the three cars roared along the very tight, narrow road. The Mercedes was still trying to pass the Bugatti, almost scraping itself along the side of the mountain, but just kicked up more dirt and dust into Samantha's face.

Suddenly she had to stamp on her brake as the three cars came slewing round a broad, sweeping bend, their cars drifting to almost the very edge of the cliff, before swinging back in and along a much wider, faster road.

The road was widening, almost wide enough for all three to run side by side, and, biting her lower lip, Samantha realised this could be her chance.

Suddenly the Bugatti hit a small rock on his racing line, the front right wheel lifting off the road as it struck. The sharp edge ripped through the rubber and steel, tearing the inner tube and instantly there was a loud bang. The tyre began to deflate, sending shards of rubber flying back into the path of the oncoming cars.

The driver fought with the wheel, but as he turned one way, the car skidded the other and he tried to compensate. The car spun, slapping the side of the mountain so hard that the steering wheel was ripped out of his hand. It instantly swerved to the other side, just missing the Mercedes, and shot off at speed into a wall of straw bales that lined the edge of the corner. His navigator grabbed the dashboard as the horror gripped him. The car tipped over the cliff edge and began to bounce as it rolled on its wheels all the way down the hill to a small plateau.

Samantha pulled the car's handbrake as she pushed the footbrake hard. The engine roared as the car skidded and shuddered along the gravelly road, as if the beast inside was escaping its skin. The wheels locked and the car slewed and slithered until the rubber bit the stone below the dust of the road and the Riley Nine came to a shuddering stop. Its engine died, the car rocking as it stalled.

Nicola threw her map onto the car floor. The two women climbed out of their car, lifting their goggles as they ran to the gap in the straw bales. Looking over the edge, Nicola cried, 'Do you think they'll be alright?'

The Bugatti was sitting in the bottom of the valley and to Samantha's eyes, everything seemed okay. They were a long way down, but the two men were still in the car and the car was still upright. As a wave of relief began to wash over her, she gripped Nicola's arm reassuringly.

'That's going to put a crimp in his race!' Samantha sighed.

She reassured Nicola as she gently rubbed her arm. 'Be alright if they can get out before it catches fire… 'She was abruptly interrupted as the Bugatti suddenly ripped itself apart. The car erupted into an inferno of orange flame and billowing, black smoke, which engulfed the whole car almost instantaneously, forcing both girls to shy away as the echo of the explosion filled the valley.

'…. Horsefeathers!'

Quickly they both ducked to one side as one of the car's wheels flew over them and bounced over their car, the cloud of billowing, black smoke drifting high into the air.

2

It was a warm, beautiful sunny day. The quiet, tall monuments of the Père Lachaise Cemetery shone like bright, rectangular mountains between the leafy lanes. The clean, marble and stone memorials, miniature manor houses along the numbered avenues with their green ornate signposts, stood like a city for the long-since departed, with their thick, snowy-silk, cobwebbed and dirty, iron- and copper-faced doors, over which now faded family names had been chiselled, each memorial adorned with crosses, stars, statues and plaques to those who had been loved. The wealthy competed with one another to create a skyline to rival the city of Paris they looked out on.

Long, sweeping roads of grey stone cobbles, with narrow dusty, gravel paths, insulated from the activities of human life, only the buzz of nature could be heard, as the songs of birds filled the treetops. A squirrel scampered from tree to tree as a bee weaved its way around the stones, sampling the nectar of the tulip flowers that blossomed in the beds along the avenues or in the minute spaces between the tightly arranged tombs.

Dressed sombrely in black, with black hats and gloves, Samantha, her bright, ginger, shingle bob shining like a halo in the sun against her black hat, her vibrant green eyes mournfully looking out through the mesh of her veil, and Nicola, fresh-faced and innocent with large blue eyes and a brunette Dutch boy hairstyle which bounced gently just off her collar, stood together along with a number of other mourners around the newly dug hole that sat between two long, polished, red granite tombs.

The group of mourners, a mixture of adults and children of all ages, comforted each other as they stood in two deep rows either side of the hole. At its foot stood a wreath on a tripod stand, with the name Pierre Gilbert embossed in gold over a green sash.

A number of the female mourners were crying into their handkerchiefs as the men stood, heads bowed, like the statues of the nearby tombs, tall and motionless. At the head of the grave stood the elderly priest in his long, white surplice, black scarf and little, black, four-peaked biretta hat with a tuft on top, reading from his prayer book. Next to him was a young altar boy holding an ornate bowl with a silver spoon and another in which was some earth.

'O God, by whose mercy the souls of the faithful find rest, mercifully grant forgiveness of their sins to thy servants and handmaids, and to all here and elsewhere who rest in Christ, that being freed from all sins, they may rejoice with thee for evermore. Through the same our Lord.'

The priest sprinkled some holy water on the coffin in the pattern of a cross. Then, while the pallbearers lifted up their ropes and together slowly lowered the mahogany coffin into the grave, the priest's young assistant handed him the small bowl with earth in it and gave the silver spoon to the woman nearest to him, the dead man's widow Sylvie, as she reached under her veil to dab a tear away from the corner of her eye.

She was about ten years older than Samantha, with blue eyes, that still seemed to sparkle from under the veil, and long blond hair that hung straight from under her hat. She was thin and an inch or so shorter than Samantha, but she maintained a cool air of dignity, not allowing her grief to overwhelm her as others in the group cried and contemplated the loss of their good friend. Sylvie took the bowl, scooped some of the soil onto the spoon and threw it into the hole onto the coffin.

There was a heavy rolling thud as it scattered over the wood. Blessing the body in turn in the name of the Lord, the mourners began to turn and walk away.

Their footsteps seemed heavy upon the gravel, as it crunched underfoot. Then, underscoring them all, there was a faster set of footsteps as Sylvie quickly came over to Samantha and Nicola, lifting her veil as she reached them.

'Thank you for coming to the funeral. I am sure if Pierre had been alive today, he would have appreciated this.' She patted Samantha gently, with warmth, on her arm.

'Doubt it!' Samantha exclaimed. 'Means we would have buried him alive!'

'Are you in a hurry to return to England? No?' Sylvie asked.

'No.' Samantha replied. 'Our train leaves tomorrow. I was thinking of taking Nicky round the Louvre. She's a Mona fan. Hasn't stopped since we got here.'

'Now I'll be able to see it for real,' Nicola added.

Samantha continued, 'And I like to keep my Nicky happy.'

They shared a quick glance and a knowing smile which was lost on Sylvie as she continued, 'Then you must come around to my house tonight. I will have my cook make you something special.'

'Thank you.' Samantha smiled warmly, patting Sylvie affectionately upon the arm.

'Shall we say about eight?' Sylvie asked.

'Sounds fine to me,' Samantha agreed.

They continued along the gravel path, their footsteps echoing together as if one step as they approached the large, high, white walls and the tall, green, iron gates at the exit of the cemetery.

'At least I take one comfort from his death,' Sylvie reassured herself as she wiped a small tear from the corner of her eye.

'What is that?' Samantha asked.

'That he died as he wanted to.'

Sylvie went a few paces ahead of them. Samantha fell back and, as she turned to her companion, Nicola asked, a little confused, 'What, screaming as he burnt to death, whilst crashing down some hillside?'

'I think she meant he died racing, which he most enjoyed,' Samantha clarified as they both caught up with Sylvie again.

'Oui,' Sylvie continued, as if she was unaware she'd been walking alone for a few paces. 'He was at his happiest when he was behind the wheel.'

They continued to walk towards the entrance as a song thrush began to sing merrily with all his heart, high in the tree above them.

*

They took the Metro back to their hotel on Avenue George V, the grand Prince de Galles, newly built in an art-deco style, timelessly elegant, a chic place at the very heart of Parisian elegance and just moments away from the Champs-Elysées, where they could stroll along marvelling at the boutiques and be near to the business district and places of cultural and historical interest such as the Arc de

Triomphe, the Trocadéro and the Eifel Tower.

Their room, one below the penthouse suites, faced into the inner court, with its balcony giving onto the square of other suites and their little balconies, all identically set with a table and two chairs looking out to the courtyard below and with the very top of the Eifel Tower peeking over the roof as if looking in on the well-to-do residents.

Their suite was divided into three rooms, with the balcony linking the lounge and the bedroom to make a square. The entrance led to a small corridor space of black tiles with a small door on the right that opened into the toilet, which had a single handbasin and bidet. On the left, a sliding set of twin doors opened into the lounge, a splendid room with a long, lounging sofa, two curved-back armchairs, a coffee table in the centre, a gas fire along the far wall and a large picture window that opened onto the balcony. It was all decorated in an electric blue with a gold sun-like clock mounted above the fireplace and its pink-and-black tiled mantel. Over the sofa there was a large painting, a cityscape of Pigalle and the Moulin Rouge at night before the War.

Straight on, the end of the corridor opened out into the bedroom, with its two single beds, vanity table, a walk-around wardrobe against the wall, two curved-back chairs and a footstool, all decorated in a style matching the living room. There was a low cupboard, on which sat a beside lamp, that originally had been between the two beds, along with two matching tables that, with their lamps, sat on the outer sides. However, the two beds had been pushed together and this lamp now sat next to the large French windows that opened out onto the balcony and, opposite them, on the other side of the beds, there was a door into the bathroom, with its large oval bath in its centre, handbasin and small, blue vanity unity that stood at the far end of what, just like the toilet, was a windowless room.

The whole room still had that freshly painted smell

and, although no expense had been spared on the sheer opulence of the surroundings, a familiar temple to the pursuit of avarice, the small additions of decoration, the figurines on the mantelpiece, the flowers on the bedroom vanity unit and the bowl of fruit in the lounge gave the suite a feeling of being a welcoming home away from home.

Samantha, now in a more casual summery dress, stood by the foot of the bed looking into a full-length mirror, next to the walk-around wardrobe, and as she pulled on her cloche hat, she called, 'So what would you like to do first, baby?'

From the balcony entered Nicola, dressed similarly, her ruby lips glistening in the bright early afternoon sun.

'We must do the Eiffel Tower first! Isn't it just the cat's pyjamas! You can see it from the balcony,' she shrieked like an excited six-year-old.

'You can see it from everywhere, well almost. It does seem to dance about a bit once you start getting near to it,' Samantha replied with a smile as Nicola looked at her via the mirror.

'I bet you can see the whole city from its observation platforms.'

'They say so,' Samantha agreed. 'It's settled then.' She tucked her ginger fringe under the rim of her hat. 'We'll do the Tower first. We'll have dinner there, just like Jules Verne, although unlike him, it's because we like the tower, not to avoid looking it and then we'll head over to the Louvre.' She turned to Nicola. 'Or we could do that tomorrow? Our train doesn't leave until six in the afternoon.'

'Well, yes, we have to see Sylvie later today so we mustn't be late,' Nicola reminded her as Samantha crossed and kissed her tenderly on her cheek, making Nicola blush a little.

'Atta girl.'

3

Sylvie was sitting on her long, ornate, gilt-and-red rococo sofa in her blue-and-white, classical, rococo lounge, which wouldn't have looked out of place in the Palace of Versailles, apart from the drinks cabinet in one corner and the gramophone in another. Her lawyer sat in an equally opulent armchair across a gold-leaf, rococo-style, coffee table with a glass top.

Her maid was pouring coffee into two small, narrow, pink cups, each of which had a white oval containing a different, highly detailed, painted image of a flower. When she'd finished pouring, she handed the cups, with their matching saucers and small golden spoons, to Sylvie and the lawyer. Their conversation continued as if the pair were oblivious to her existence.

'The weather's been nice today, considering.'

'Yes,' her lawyer agreed. 'It was nice to see so many of

Pierre's friends, especially his fellow racers.'

Sylvie took her cup and sipped her coffee before replying.

'Yes, it was very good of them to come.'

Her maid curtseyed slightly and then left them as her lawyer continued.

'It's just a shame what I have to tell you next is so…. bad.'

'Bad?' She asked suspiciously. 'But surely, I have no worries? Pierre was a very wealthy man? No?'

'You are right, Madame. No,' he replied.

'No?' She couldn't believe it. He had to be mistaken.

'It seems that Pierre,' he continued after a quick sip of his drink, 'albeit a great racing driver, was in fact also a great gambler with a very bad head for business. All the shares he has in corporations have lost their value, so that they are almost worthless. Well, those who haven't already gone bust and, what with his debts from racing, you are, I'm sad to say, Madame, broke.' He took another sip of his coffee as she waited in stunned silence. 'Even this house is leased. Fortunately, that's been paid, so you won't have to leave until that expires in forty-five years' time, but otherwise, Madame, you are, I repeat, broke.'

'But he always had money?' She was still stunned, like her whole world had just been dragged out through the pit of her stomach and ripped from her soul. She was cold and numb. It was like she was watching someone else's life, performed in a strange foreign language as nothing seemed to make sense.

'Yes.' The lawyer sighed. 'How?' he asked. 'I cannot say where that came from. There are no details as to where it came from in his accounts. He never earned from any shares and yet he always paid his bills on time, twice a year! I've looked hard through his papers, Madame, but the fact is it seems he only left you with the Cœur d'Or.'

'I know he was always very generous, especially as a lover, but I suppose it's better to remembered for something endearing.'

'No, Madame.' He coughed discreetly. 'He brought it in '25, in Dublin.'

'Dublin, in '25, that…' She was even more confused. 'That was the year before we were married? Yes, I remember now. He and some friends went to Belgium as a sort of last cycling holiday together before we wed. But I do not recall him saying they went to Ireland as well.'

'Alas, so it is.' He drank some more of his coffee and relaxed back into his chair. 'Of all his assets, it's the only one he had paid for outright from the start. As far as we can tell, he's never hired it out and he certainly has never sold it, or done anything with it, but now, Madame, it's yours.' She sipped her coffee as he wondered if he should have a cigarette now or wait until he'd left. Noticing how confused she looked, he added, 'Maybe he bought this for you as a surprise?'

'What is it?' Sylvie asked taking another sip of her coffee. She was beginning to get over the shock and was already thinking over a way to keep herself afloat and to enjoy the lifestyle she was now accustomed to.

'Madame?' He replied.

'What he left this, what is it, object?' She asked. She was beginning to think, though it was still all unclear. At least now she could focus. The shock of everything in her world being turned upside down was at last coming back into view.

'A small pleasure yacht, currently moored in Torquay.'

'Where?' she asked. She'd never heard of such a place in all of France.

'It's a harbour in England, Madame.'

'A yacht?'

He nodded and sipped his coffee. The cigarette would have to wait.

'But he didn't like to be on the water?' She questioned the sense of this, but then nothing seemed so strange anymore. 'He was always fond of the car! He was always so anti-water that he wouldn't even have any in his Scotch!'

'What can I say? Shall I send someone to England to inspect it and see what sort of a price we can get for it?'

She paused to think for a moment, then she began to relax and smiled as she dropped back into the rich padding of her sofa.

'No need. Our friend Mademoiselle Bishop and her friend Mademoiselle White, they are from England. They will be able to look at this boat for me and sell it for me.'

'Very good, Madame.'

He placed his empty cup back down on the tray.

*

Standing by the edge of the highest observation platform of the biscuit-bronze Eiffel Tower looking down over the city from the corner of the Champ de Mars and the river Seine, Samantha, her arm in Nicola's, gazed down the 1,063 feet from Paris's tallest structure and through the faint, wispy mist haze to the bustling flotilla of small crafts inching their way along the river. In the distance, the busy cars, trams, and horse-drawn carts, clattered and roared along the city's cobbled streets.

There was a slight breeze so high up, making Samantha wish she'd brought her fox-fur stole as she felt a little chilly around her neck and she reminded herself that sometimes it was warmer in London than even down in the south of France, especially in springtime.

'It's a beautiful city.' Nicola sighed affectionately. 'Reminds me of… Gateshead. But without the chimneys.'

'I know what you mean,' Samantha agreed. 'You can only really appreciate the beauty of a city when you can see it from up high.'

'Maybe they should build a tower like this in London? Or maybe an apartment block?' Nicola mused.

'Who would want to live in an apartment block in the clouds?' Samantha asked. 'Anyway, London's a busy town, not so tidy as this and with the smoke, fog and bad weather, living in the clouds would be about right in London.' She grinned to herself as she added, 'No. Only a fool would want to live in a tall building as high as this in London, because for most the year, all you would be able to see are clouds and who wants to look at nothing but cold, grey clouds all day?'

They began to walk around the narrow platform.

'Why don't you live in Paris?' Nicola asked.

'I like Paris,' Samantha admitted. 'I was schooled here, in a boarding school until I was fifteen, but, although I enjoyed my education here, for most of that time, life was hard back then. Suppose now that Paris is just so gay once again, what with all these Americans living here, writing, painting and so forth, it might be worth thinking about moving back for a while? If things change back home and London stops being so gay, then let's do it. Let's rent a house overlooking the Parc Montsouris. I quite like it there. You know, it was created under Napoléon III and inspired by parks in London. He's buried in St Michael's Abbey, Farnborough. Or we could live near here, the Champ de Mar, then we would be able to walk to the Eifel Tower every morning after getting our bread. Be ab-so-lute-ly the cat's meow.' Nicola smiled as Samantha added thoughtfully, 'But I think in my heart, if I had to leave the good old British Isles for any real length of time I might move to the Netherlands. Say like, Amsterdam.'

'Amsterdam? Why?' Nicola frowned, bemused.

'No hills!' Samantha exclaimed as she explained. 'I wouldn't have to keep stretching the handbrake cable on my poor old Alvis, no need to ever have to do a wretched hill start ever again!' Samantha looked at her watch. 'Though maybe Sweden would be better?' She questioned her own thought adding, 'At least they drive on the left-hand side of the road, not like these French. No wonder they keep crashing around that Arc de Triomphe. They're all approaching it from the wrong direction!' She nodded towards the lift. 'Let's have a bite to eat and set off back to the hotel to get ready for Sylvie's.'

Nicola nodded and arm in arm they headed over to the waiting lift.

4

That evening, the taxi took Samantha and Nicola to the four-floor town house on the edge of the Bois de Boulogne. Set in a street of similar properties, Sylvie's house was of the old Napoleon the Third style, Haussmann-designed, sandstone with a blue slate roof.

The front door was central and the front garden was very short, protected by a black, iron railing fence. The ground and second floor windows were more gothic, with rounded arches but the first and the third, the attic floor, with its window standing proud of the roof itself, were rectangular.

As the house was on the corner of the street, there was an electric street lamp shining its harsh white light on them as they stepped out. After Samantha paid the taxi driver, arm in arm the two women quickly skipped up the four steps to the front door and pulled the long bell rod beside the large black door.

They were met by Sylvie's butler and shown to the lounge, but it wasn't until later, at dinner, that the more formal proceedings of the evening began to unveil themselves.

It was a large cavernous room, with a long table in the centre around which twelve could easily have sat, decorated with the Napoleonic bee-patterned wallpaper and a sideboard to one side near the door. It was otherwise quite spartan. There was a large crystal chandelier hanging from the centre of the ceiling, and two candelabras on the table, but only the one nearest them was actually lit, and on the other two walls hung three huge canvases, each depicting rural 17th century France.

Sylvie was at the head, with Samantha and Nicola sitting opposite each other, one place down from Sylvie. The claret in their expensive crystal glasses sparkled like red rubies in the candlelight as the three of them enjoyed their lamb cutlets.

'Of course we'd both be more than happy to take a look at this boat for you,' Samantha replied, putting her knife down to pick up her glass of wine. 'Daddy has a small cottage near there. And I'm sure Daddy knows someone who would want to buy it. He has some pretty swell connections really. Or if you wish, we could sail it back to France for you!'

'I've never been to Torquay!' Nicola added and Samantha replied, 'You'll love it! They've got some wonderful sea down south for fishing.'

'Strange!' Sylvie was puzzled. 'My Pierre was never the one for fishing! He was one for the taste of the cock, would you not agree?'

'Ab-so-lute-ly,' Samantha replied, then, noticing the look of surprise etched across Nicola's face, adding, 'Chickens slow-roasted, with vegetables or braised in red wine, was all Pierre would eat when he was racing.'

'But I thought you said it was all fishing down south?'

Nicola was confused.

'It is.' Samantha replied and sipped her wine.

'Incredible.' Sylvie took a sip of her wine. 'I still cannot believe that he has… had a boat. I never once saw him show any interest in the sea. It was hard enough to make him have a bath. Once a month, whether he needed it or not! So why would he have a boat? And why in England? I did not know he ever raced there? So why would he have a boat there?'

'Don't know.' Samantha shrugged. 'But I'm sure we'll find out once we've had a look at it,' Samantha assured her as Sylvie replied with a little nod in agreement.

'That is enough talk about my husband's affairs.' She put her wine glass down, as if to underline this, like an auctioneer bringing down his gavel.

'Thought we were talking about his boat?' Nicola whispered across the table to Samantha, who responded with a whimsical smile.

'Shall we have our coffees in the conservatory?' Sylvie asked.

Nicola nodded as Samantha turned to Sylvie, replying, 'And how! It's such a nice night.'

*

It was a bright sunny day in Paris, not a cloud in the sky. The rooftops shimmered and the river seemed to sparkle as if it was made of crystal.

The lobby of the hotel, Prince de Galles, was a large, open space with a sweeping staircase to the right, midway between the brass revolving door and the long, teak reception desk that faced it. The floor was polished brown marble, with a white marble patterned inlay. The walls were matching colours and patterns and the ceiling was high and white. Behind the stairs were the two brass doors of the lifts and in the centre of the lobby there was a small arrangement of seating dispersed between the potted palm trees and the two tables on which a number of magazines and newspapers were laid out for anyone waiting for a guest to read.

There was a small corridor next to the end of the reception desk that led round to the tearoom and the dining room as well as to the other reception rooms with the blue-coated staff ever on hand to attend to any guests' needs.

Samantha was standing by the reception. The man behind the counter, tall and suave with a fine, chiselled jaw, handed over her receipt, as Nicola appeared from the lift, pulling her light coat loosely about her. She glanced around the lobby and then seeing her companion, she came over to Samantha, who met her in the middle of the lobby.

'Luggage has gone ahead, our train leaves for Dover in six hours, we'll be on the Calais night ferry, where we'll meet the rail connection, and Albert will meet us in London. I've sent the telegram so we can't change our minds now.'

'Swell,' Nicola replied with a broad smile.

'Which gives us enough time to see the Mona Lisa if we can get past all those people crowding around it! You'd think they'd hung Marlene Dietrich there, the way they behave! Then I thought we would have a quiet bite before we head back to England.'

'Ab-so-lute-ly.' Nicola agreed. They briefly touched hands as if they were about to hold them, when suddenly becoming self-conscious, aware that they were not alone, they stopped and instead turned to make their way over to the lobby exit. The doorman held the door next to the revolving doors open for them and they left the hotel stepping out onto the busy street.

5

'Do you know she hasn't got any eyebrows?'

Samantha took a closer look, leaning slightly over the red-velvet rope in front of the painting.

'You know baby, you're right.' She turned to Nicola, 'Maybe it was never finished?'

'Or badly restored over the centuries?' Nicola sighed.

'Might explain her enigmatic smile?' Samantha smiled, turning to Nicola with admiration, 'You have a keen eye for art.'

'It used to be a hobby of mine. I used to paint a lot when I was young, watercolours mainly, mostly of the docks, but it was something I loved to do with my free time.'

'Remind me when we get back to London to buy you some art supplies, we could have Albert make us up a hamper and we could easily make it to the coast in my

Alvis for a spot of painting on a sunny day.'

Nicola said nothing, as a large smile stretched across her lips and moved away to look at the rest of the artwork in the room. That was so typical of Samantha, so generous towards her, that at times she felt unworthy of such attention and often wished she could be as generous in return.

She looked closely at the other paintings.

These works were magnificent as well, but nothing in the room was as popular as La Joconde, or the Mona Lisa as Nicola knew her, painted by Leonardo da Vinci.

It was a half-length portrait painting, in oil on a white wooden panel, thought to be of Lisa Gherardini, the wife of Francesco Del Giocondo, sitting bolt upright in a pozzetto armchair with her arms folded, right hand on left, her gaze fixed on the observer. She appeared alive to an unusual extent, by the way Leonardo had soft blended the lines between the colours creating an ambiguous mood, especially in the corners of her mouth, and the corners of her eyes.

She was depict sitting in front of an imaginary landscape, seated in an open loggia with dark pillar bases on either side. Behind her a vast landscape receded to icy mountains, where winding paths and a distant bridge gave only the slightest hint of any other human presence and with the clever use of an aerial perspective, the horizon line was level with her eyes, which linked the figure with the landscape, emphasizing the overall mysterious nature, which like Lisa's expression, could only be, as frequently described, somewhat enigmatic.

'Well now that we've seen it,' Samantha glanced at her watch as she crossed over to where Nicola was now standing, 'shall we go and get something to eat?'

Nicola smiled, 'And how, sounds just swell.'

*

Leaving The Louvre and keeping in mind Nicola's delicate stomach and the train journey ahead, they had a light meal at a small Bistro Samantha knew well along the south bank of the river Seine overlooking the Notre-Dame cathedral. Coquilles St Jacques, sole meunière, salade niçoise, and a new desert that had become all the rage, a citrus stuffed pancake flambé in cognac called a crepes suzette, which Samantha thought was so nice, she was going to have Albert give it a go when they arrived back in London.

Though for all their adventures in food that day, not for all the wine in France could Samantha tempt Nicola to try the snails, then once the wine was drunk and after they'd had a small coffee, they took a taxi to meet their luggage the hotel had forwarded to the Paris Gare du Nord to catch the train bound for Calais Fréthun and from there the ferry to England.

Soon they were speeding across the flat French countryside, the steam from the large engine wafting past, occasionally obscuring their view, as they raced against the setting sun casting its long shadows over hedgerows and tree-lined fields. They both relaxed, chilled champagne in hand, their minds and thoughts turning back to home.

*

The hours passed, then through customs and on to the ferry, its two huge funnels of thick smoke fogging the upper deck as, out of the harbour and out onto the choppy sea, the plucky vessel rode the white rolling waves.

The ferry, lurched left, lurched right, as down in the bar, listening to the small quintet playing softly against the moans of those whose sea legs had deserted them, Samantha and Nicola sat by themselves at a small round table. Nicola was reading her book, on the table in front of her a little green-coloured box of travel sickness pills she'd bought back in Paris, in easy reach in case she needed some more. Her eyes never darted off the page, except each time the ferry lurched wildly and she felt her stomach heavy, she'd quickly glance over to the packet of pills, but after a glance from Samantha and a deep breath, her stomach would simmer down and she would go back to staring hard at the page until the next wave struck.

Meanwhile, Samantha read a French newspaper, totally at ease with everything, as she sat quietly ignoring the motion of the boat. They each had a cocktail and a cold-meat sandwich and were oblivious to the rest of the world as gamely onward the little ferry carried them over towards the reassuring White Cliffs of Dover.

However, Samantha wasn't settled. She was only half reading the news articles as in the back of her mind she was wondering why Pierre had bought a boat and why he had moored it in England. She could have understood if he had moored it in Italy or France, the two countries he mainly raced in.

He had been, at least it seemed, a bit of a rough diamond, a cheeky rough, not really interested in anything other than winning the race, and playing up to the ladies. In '23 when she had been racing away from Brooklands for a few months in Italy and France, he had spent the whole time trying to chat her up, boasting how wonderful he was in bed and that she was wasting a once in a lifetime opportunity by not sleeping with him.

He was a right charmer, if you liked that mild bad-boy image, but he was still a lifetime opportunity she was glad to have avoided, albeit, she had still enjoyed his company all the same. She loved to listen to his wild anecdotes during those exhausting nights at the bar. He was like her, a wild spirit, and like her, he knew how to party. There was nothing too shameful, she remembered. He had always been seen with two dollies on his arms leaving the casino. Well before he married Sylvie that was. Since they had wed, he had given up the dollies, well, in public at least, but not the casino. He was famous for his gambling as much as his skill as a driver.

But like Sylvie had said, he wasn't one for boats. She could agree it would have been more like him to have several cars, not a yacht. The only reason he would have any kind of boat she could work out was if he wanted a cheap place to live in whilst racing, but as he had always stayed in the hotels with casinos, it was most unlikely he would have bought the boat to live on during the racing season and as he had never raced in Britain or Ireland, the whole thing seemed even more strange.

Then an idea occurred to her. Maybe it was to have been a love nest for some relationship he was planning before he got married. Yes, she convinced herself. It had to be something very simple. After all, Pierre may have been may things but complicated was not one of them.

She was able to relax, enjoy her sandwich, read the paper and dream about sleeping in her own bed for a week.

*

Soon they were in Dover and quickly through the customs checks. From there, as they raced against the rising sun, they sped through the leafy English countryside, the steam from the large engine wafting past, occasionally obscuring their view as they trundled through valleys and tunnels, past towns and miles upon miles of farmland, both open fields and orchards, until at last, it all gave way to a more industrial landscape and the familiar world both girls knew well. London.

6

The swirls of smoke disappeared up into the high glass roof, which was supported by ornate ironwork with its intricate leaf filigree. Everywhere was the shrieking noise of the steam whistles, the choking taste of the bitter steam, the smell of coal and the sparks from the chimneys as the engines came to life and hauled themselves away from the black platforms. All around, through every hole and crevice, their smoke drifted past the apple-and-cream coloured wood, over the waiting rooms and ticket gates and up high, higher than the Roman numeral clock at the far end of the concourse.

Throughout the station people rushed about in this anthill of activity. Working people, late to get to the office scurried past other commuters, as porters with long, flat barrows pushed the mail and other goods onto the trains, some taking goods and cases off, filling their barrows so high that they were stacked too high to see over. Everything from newspapers and cases to meat, fish and vegetables was coming off and being loaded onto the carts, trucks and vans to be taken to the city's various markets, all accompanied by a cacophony of noise which erupted like a discordant percussion section, harsh and brash metallic and industrial, almost robotic like the evolving world outside.

Samantha and Nicola entered this throng, a porter following, pushing his sack barrow piled high with their luggage as they came along the concourse. Near the entrance stood Albert, an average-looking man, with a quiet sense of dignity about him, in his long, black coat and matching bowler hat. He had short, salt-and-pepper hair and was in his forties. Perched across the bridge of his nose he wore a pair of round, brown Bakelite spectacles. On seeing them, he gave a discreet wave. They spotted him and led the porter over.

'Pleasant trip, Miss?' he asked politely with a genuine feeling of quiet interest, as, of all those he had ever worked for over the years, Samantha was his favourite.

'Ab-so-lute-ly,' Samantha replied warmly.

'I have the Riley parked just outside, Miss.' He then beckoned to the porter, who, after a little sigh, picked up the handles to the sack barrow once more and putting his weight behind it, pushed the dozen or so heavy cases again.

'Has anything important happened whilst we were away?' Samantha asked as they turned and began to walk slowly towards the station's main exit.

'Lord Tobias Delevingne came round,' Albert answered. 'I put him up for a couple of nights in your spare room, though I did inform him that Miss White would be returning with you and so he's spending the next couple of nights at his club before heading down to see his parents in Hereford, Miss. I think he was under the misapprehension that Miss White would require the room.'

'For the time being let's keep it that way.' Samantha grinned. 'That way we don't have to be on our best behaviour.'

'Speak for yourself!' Nicola exclaimed. 'I'm always at my best.'

'Ab-so-lute-ly baby, but sometimes it's best not to advertise.' Samantha turned to Albert. 'I suppose our cellar-smeller has been burning the blue flame at our expense?'

'I have to confess to a small lie, Miss,' Albert coughed embarrassedly. 'I did inform the gentleman that you kept the key to the cabinet, though I did take the liberty of ordering some more wine, which they say they will deliver tomorrow.'

'Thank you, Albert.'

She let Albert and the porter go ahead of her as she slipped her arm in Nicola's and they dropped back a couple of paces.

'When we get back, we'll have a bath, some supper and unpack, then pack afresh for Torquay.'

'And how.' Nicola agreed.

The brown Riley Monaco, with its darker brown, hard roof, was a boxy looking car with a long, black running board connecting the matching back and front wings. The two headlights were slightly proud of the wings, though connected via a bar across the front of the tall radiator. There was a spare wheel at the back, and a boot that opened out to create a chute for the luggage.

The main body of the car was similar to a small horse-drawn coach, with the engine bolted to the front over the front wheels, and had a long, tan, back-bench seat, that was firmly padded in the rear and in the front two similar single seats, with slightly curved backs for the comfort of the driver and passenger, but unlike any prestigious saloon car, there was no dividing partition between the front and back.

The Riley was parked by the kerb directly before the

main entrance and as Albert stood by, supervising the porter while he placed the cases carefully, Samantha and Nicola remained a few paces back watching both of them.

'Albert?' Samantha asked. He turned to her.

'Yes, Miss?'

'When we get home, will you draw a bath for Miss White and myself, please?'

'I'm afraid at this time of day, Miss, there will only be sufficient hot water for one bath.'

The two girls looked at each other and a cheeky smile crept across Nicola's lips.

'That's alright, Albert,' Samantha replied, a devilish twinkle in her eyes. 'We'll share.'

Just then the porter lost his grip on the large case he was lifting and it fell to the floor. Very embarrassed, he quickly picked it up.

*

The kitchen to Samantha's house was little more than a white rectangular room, with the sink under the main window and next to it, facing the entrance door there was a door that led to the scullery and the back door to a small yard which opened out onto the small coal bunker. Next to the door into the house there was a large Welsh dresser with all the pots and pans for cooking nestled on its shelves and under the sink there was a curtained area of shelves below which all the cleaning equipment was kept.

The larder was between the scullery door and the sink, kept cool by being next to the back door with two of its single-skinned walls exposed to the elements and on the wall opposite the Welsh dresser there was the stove. Taking up the most space amongst all this, there was a large pine table on which all the meals could be prepared.

On the wall side opposite the window there was another narrow table on which some of the electrical gadgets stood, including the black, square, double toaster, which was softly buzzing away as it browned one side of the two slices of bread clasped up against the elements.

Albert waited, a tray readied on the table with tea and breakfast plates for two. When he decided that those sides had browned sufficiently, he opened down the sides of the toaster in turn, took off the slices, turned them round so that the white side faced the elements and then shut them again before taking the kettle from the hot stove to fill the large teapot with hot water.

Soon after, he turned off the toaster, removed the slices of toast, both sides now brown, and cut them into triangles before placing them in the toast rack and then placed that on the tray. Taking the tray, he left the kitchen.

He made his way along the corridor carrying the tray carefully as Nicola, barefoot and still in her pyjamas came down the stairs.

'Morning, Miss.'

'Morning, Albert.'

He placed the tray down on the table next to the door at the foot of the stairs and held open the dining-room door, letting her enter first. Then he picked up the tray and after a pause followed her in.

There was a gentle creak of the floorboards as into the room came Nicola. Samantha was already sitting at the table, one down from the top, still dressed in her pyjamas, eating her breakfast as Nicola sat opposite her. Albert entered, crossed over to the sideboard and placed the tray next to the hotplate warming the scrambled eggs, bacon, sausages, kidneys, tomatoes, mushrooms and the terrine of porridge, before bringing over the toast and tea to Nicola's place and then returning to fetch her some porridge.

'Albert?' Samantha asked, after taking a quick sip of her tea. 'I think we'll make a long weekend of it down in Torquay. Will you pack our golf things as well, please? I think Daddy's spare set will do for Nicky.'

Nicola grimaced slightly.

'Very good, Miss.'

'Won't we have to be members to play a round?' Nicola asked, still a little tired from the journey back from France as she felt she had woken an hour too early.

'We don't have to be members to play. If you have the right gear, anyone can play. We'll buy visitors' passes,' Samantha assured her. 'Daddy does it all the time when he's away on business. He says it's much cheaper then joining every course in the country.'

Nicola smiled uneasily and poured her tea.

'I just hope we have some glorious weather.' Samantha sighed. 'They have some of the most wonderful beaches you'll see anywhere in the British Isles.' She began to put some marmalade on the corner of a slice of toast and then cut it from the main slice, adding quickly as if it was an afterthought, 'That reminds me. Albert, you'd better pack our swimming costumes too.'

He placed the porridge down before Nicola.

'As you wish, Miss, but if you intend to spend some time on the beach, will you get to play a round?'

'Only if it's quiet and secluded!' she reassured him.

'Yes, Miss.' Then took his place by the wall near to the head of the table. 'Will that be all, Miss?'

Samantha turned to Nicola who replied with a small nod that she was content. Then she turned back to Albert.

'That will be all, thank you.'

He returned a discreet nod and then quietly left as Nicola remarked.

'Torquay sounds the bee's knees!'

'Oh, my word. It's totally copacetic,' Samantha replied. 'And if this boat of Sylvie's is in dock, we might be able to take her out for a quick sail. I doubt it's much of a boat. I suspect Pierre bought it for some doll he picked up before he met Sylvie. That's probably why it's still in Torquay. I half expect when we get there, it's going to cost us more money to make her seaworthy and pay those harbour fees that it will be worth.'

'Oh, I hope not. After the week Sylvie's had, she

needs some good news.'

'I agree, but to be honest, baby, Pierre was never the smartest bimbo in the world. He was only good at three things, although I only have his word for one of them, and none of them had anything to do with the sea. I wouldn't be surprised when we get there; we find that the Cœur d'Or's not even got a mast.'

7

The early morning sun shone brightly against the flat exterior of the row of three-storey town houses along the quiet mews. About three quarters of the way along the terrace, down the steps from the blue front door with its brass house number, 27, over its lion-head knocker, sat the Riley.

There were a small number of trees planted on the opposite side of the road and birds could be heard singing.

Albert, dressed like a chauffeur, in a long, grey, double-breasted coat and matching peaked cap, stood by the rear passenger door, the Riley's engine already running, as from the house emerged Samantha and Nicola, now dressed in short dresses and cloche hats.

Samantha closed the door firmly and set the deadbolt. Quickly they ran together down to Albert, who opened the door, which opened out from the centre of the car. As they climbed in, Samantha paused.

'You'll be alright up front on your own, won't you, Albert?' she asked. 'Think I'll join Nicky in the struggle buggy.'

'Right you are, Miss.'

She climbed in and he closed the door before making his way around to the driver's side. There was a dull clunking noise as he found the gear and then released the handbrake. Slowly with a slight jerk forward, the Riley pulled away.

*

By nightfall they were trundling along the narrow country road, with its high steep banks etched out in the yellow light of the Riley's headlamps. The torrential rain lashed down on them, slowing their progress and making the single wiper squeal as it raced from side to side across the windscreen, each stroke clearing, just for a moment, an oval space in the glass before the water blurred everything in front of them once more.

Albert was driving slowly, peering through the blurred screen into the dark, when suddenly, seeing the road opening out to a crossroads, he was forced to brake, the drums hissing in protest. The car slid to a gentle stop.

Gently he pulled on the handbrake as he stared across to the small square of ground on which the tall, white post with its four pointing fingers stood.

Taking the bullseye lamp out from the pocket in the side of his door, he switched it on. Opening the door, he braced himself against the weather, wrapped tightly inside his grey coat, as he stepped out into the harsh wind and the torrents of the monsoon.

His boots splashed though the puddles near to the verge. Squinting into the wind, holding the coat tightly around his neck, Albert shone the light up at the sign, quickly reading all four destinations before he swiftly clambered back into the car.

He closed his door firmly and drew deep a gasping breath before wiping the water away from his eyes. Samantha stubbed out her cigarette into her silver-and-rosewood travel ashtray and, as she snapped its lid shut, she leant forward.

'Are we there?'

'Not yet, Miss.' He shuddered, feeling a little cold as an icy droplet slipped inside the collar of his coat. 'Only another five miles. It's the bad weather. I couldn't make out the sign through all the water on the windscreen.'

She gently patted Albert on the shoulder to reassure him as she sat back with Nicola, who was fast asleep under the travel rug, her head resting against the side window.

'Summer's finally here then,' Samantha remarked, pulling her half of the rug more tightly around her waist.

'That's correct, Miss.' He pulled the lever back into gear with the familiar clunk and then let the handbrake go. The car pulled away, taking the left turning.

*

It was still raining an hour later when they reached the cottage. It was like the clouds had kept pace with them all the way. Illuminated by the headlights, the cottage, which stood alone in a small hedged-off garden overlooking some rolling fields, was small. Whitewashed, with a window in each corner around the door, which was framed by creeping honeysuckle, and with a steep thatched roof, but without a light on inside or any smoke from the chimney, the cottage seemed cold and soulless as it was ravaged by the storm.

Slowly the Riley pulled up just a few yards from the door and shuddered for a moment. Its engine died as Albert opened and closed his door before rushing over to the cottage and unlocking it. Then he splashed back through the shallow, muddy puddles to open the rear car door for both Nicola and Samantha to dash inside past him.

He closed the car door and then, after pulling his peaked cap down more over his eyes, he quickly nipped round to back of the car, trying to avoid as many of the puddles as he could, to start unloading the luggage.

*

Sam stood in the middle of the room as, by the door, Nicola turned on the light and the cosy-looking living room lit up before them.

There was a small fireplace with a little mantel over it and the sofa and two armchairs were nice and plump looking under their heavily floral pattern covers. There was a mirror on the mantel, a painting of a boat at sea on the chimney breast, a small coffee table by the fireplace, a dresser on the long wall as they entered, and, on the wall opposite, there was another door next to the foot of the open staircase.

'Not too bad,' Samantha commented to herself as Nicola passed her and opened the far door.

'There's a kitchen in here. Oh, and a kettle!' She peered through. 'Shall I make us a cup of tea?'

'Ab-so-lute-ly.' Samantha agreed as Nicola smiled and disappeared into the kitchen. Samantha looked at the open fireplace, then at the coal in the bucket beside it. She sighed heavily as she assured herself, 'Albert can do that when he's finished. After all, that's more his sort of thing anyway!'

The door whipped open as Albert entered carrying all their cases. He pushed it shut behind him as he spoke.

'I'll just unpack yours and Miss White's luggage then I'll start supper.'

'Very good, Albert,' she agreed, quickly adding, 'Oh, and could you light this fire as well?'

'Certainly, Miss,' he replied as he staggered across the

room and awkwardly made his way up the stairs.

She removed her hat and sat down on the chair that had its back to the door. Just then Nicola appeared in the doorway, leaning against the jamb. She smiled and Samantha, her smile beaming back, couldn't help but feel glad she was there on this adventure with her.

Not that it was going to be much of an adventure. An hour or two to decide what to do with Sylvie's boat, then a few days enjoying the beaches, the seafood and the local golf courses, but still, after the events of the past few weeks, she was glad to be away from the same old faces of London and have the time to reflect on life. She knew they would mean well, trying to help her forget about Pierre, but cocktails and parties would only delay her sadness, and deep down, she did still feel a great sadness in his loss.

Yet Nicola, just by standing there, with the flickering light from the range behind her, shimmering like some aura all around her, keeping her company, made Samantha feel the sadness wasn't all consuming, wasn't tearing her mind apart, making her feel guilty that she hadn't driven off that cliff or died in the fireball.

It wasn't something that had tainted her love of the sport before, seeing friends die. She'd seen death before, many times during the war, albeit, some of them had been from starvation, some coming back from the front and worst of all, those killed in the Zeppelin raids. Back then, she'd lived with death daily.

When the war was only a few miles away, when you could hear the cannon fire from your bed, the horrors of war were constant, so seeing friends coming off the bank at Brooklands or other circuits and dying hadn't stopped her.

Being a reckless adventurer back then had kept her going. Only the adulation and the desire to be the best has spurred her on. The exhilaration and the feeling that every bend could be her last had excited her, made her feel more alive than she had ever been before but now, looking into her angel's eyes, she realised that it had all changed.

She felt there was more to life, more to lose, her angel. There was a fear there, not for herself, but that she might cause this feeling of sadness and pain in Nicola. It all seemed so insignificant, that adventure, that lust for fame and glory compared to what she had now.

'I've put enough water in for three. I'm sure Albert's going to need a drink after all that driving.'

'Ab-so-lute-ly,' Samantha agreed.

'Do you think we should make an early start tomorrow?'

'Yes.' Samantha nodded. 'We should try and get to the harbour no later than eleven.'

8

The next day was warm and bright with a very slight breeze. Birds were singing and bees were already buzzing around the roses in the back garden and through the honeysuckle. The ground water was still pooled in a couple of places, but largely the ground was as dry as an old sun-bleached bone.

In the main bedroom, as the sunlight steamed through the thin, pale-green curtain onto the head of the bed, Samantha, with Nicola spooning behind her, lay fast asleep.

Softly, the door opened with a gentle creak as Albert entered carrying a small tray with two cups, the milk already in them, and a small, silver, electroplated teapot. He carefully made his way around the foot of the bed, carefully avoiding the wardrobe that almost blocked off the room in the corner where it met the window wall, and placed it down on the night table next to Samantha before leaving and closing the door behind him as silently as he'd arrived.

A bird started to chirp on the windowsill as Samantha began to wake. Rubbing the sleep from her eyes, she slipped round onto her other side and for a moment she lay there, watching Nicola breathing gently, her eyes still closed as she slept.

Gently and quietly Samantha slipped from under the blankets and padded barefoot across to the window and let the curtain slip back along the brass rail, its brass rings scraping with a hollow, metallic echo as the sunlight began to stream in.

She then padded back over to the bed. She noticed that on one of the saucers there was a sugar cube, and so poured her own tea in the other cup, leaving the other one, before heading back to the window to look out over the rolling hills and clifftops to the sea beyond.

Nicola began to stir so Samantha turned back to her.

'Morning, baby. Tea?'

She went back as Nicola sat up and plumped the pillow behind her for support.

'Please.'

Samantha began to pour Nicola a tea adding, 'I'll just see if Albert's started breakfast. It's a lovely day. If it stays fine, I'm sure we'll be able to have a look at this boat of Sylvie's very quickly and then spend an hour or two down on the beach before lunch.'

'And how,' Nicola agreed and took her cup to cradle in her hands, before dropping the sugar cube into her cup.

'I'll tell Albert to pack the primus.' Samantha finished her tea, placing her cup down on the tray, while Nicola stirred hers. Then, as Samantha left her, Nicola took a quick sip and relaxed, listening to the bird that was back on the windowsill singing his heart out.

As Samantha came down the stairs, she could see Albert was placing their breakfast settings on the folding table by the lounge window.

'I was about to call you, Miss.' He turned to her. 'But I see you're up already.'

'Must be the sea air.' She shrugged. 'I feel all invigorated, just like being on the edge!'

'Very good, Miss. Tea or coffee?' he asked.

'I think a cup of Joe today,' she replied. 'We've a lot to do. We've got to go down to the harbour.'

'Very good, Miss.' He bowed before heading off to the kitchen just as Nicola began to make her way down the stairs. Samantha crossed over to the breakfast table and took her seat, with her back to the fireplace.

'Albert's making coffee. Is that fine with you, baby?' she asked as Nicola reached the foot of the stairs.

'Ab-so-lute-ly.' She yawned pulling her gown tighter over her nightdress.

Samantha glanced over the table. Apart from their plates and clean cups, in the centre there was a rack of toast, a butter dish, and two pots, one of jam, the other was some clear honey. She turned the nearer of the two, the honey, towards her and read the paper label, glued slightly askew.

'Ow, we've got some local honey.' She picked the jar up and began to unscrew the lid to smell it. 'Albert's a one. He must have gone down to the shops early. He's the berries.' Then she took her knife and smeared some honey on her toast as Nicola yawned again and sat opposite her.

Albert entered with the coffee pot and placed it on the coffee table between the armchairs.

'If you are both ready, Miss, Miss.' He looked at them both in turn. 'I'll bring in breakfast. I afraid it's not up to usual standard. I've only been able to cook some bacon, eggs, mushrooms, kidneys, tomatoes and the toast. Sorry, but there's no porridge or grape-nuts, Miss.'

'That's fine, Albert. That will be fine.'

He left to the kitchen returning almost instantly with their plates which he placed before them.

'I apologise for taking the liberty of not allowing you to help yourself, Miss, but there's no sideboard.'

'That's fine, Albert,' Samantha reassured him.

'If that's all, Miss?' he asked. 'I'll quickly clean the Riley before we head down to the harbour.'

'Thank you,' Samantha replied, as with a nod like a bow, Albert returned to the kitchen as Nicola slipped out from her seat and crossed over to the coffee table to fetch the coffee pot.

'Would you like me to put some honey on your toast too, baby?' Samantha asked.

'Ab-so-lute-ly,' she replied as she returned and started to pour some coffee in to both their cups.

Samantha dipped the honey spoon into the jar, twirled it around once in the jar and kept the stem turning in her hand as she lifted it out and then, as she held the spoon over the toast, from its ridges the honey then began to trickle down on to the toast.

She put some more honey on her own toast, before putting the spoon down. Nicola returned with the coffee pot to the table and after setting it down, Nicola picked up a slice of toast. She took a large bite as Samantha smiled and watched her eat, cradling her cup in her hands a moment before taking a small sip.

'The golf course is on the other side of the bay,' Samantha began. 'We should be able to get a few holes in later and maybe play a round tomorrow?'

'I have to admit I'm a bit of a Dumb Dora when it comes to golf.' Nicola sighed, wiping a dribble of honey from her chin. 'I've never played it before. Though my father's a doctor, his practice is on the poor side of town, by the docks and sometimes, it's hard to get the money you're owned when the patient sets sail for Arkhangelsk.'

'Not to worry baby, we'll soon know what your handicap is.'

'Hitting the ball!' Nicola sighed.

'It's all about your swing.' Samantha smiled. 'Don't

worry. I'll help you swing, baby.'

*

The Harbour Master was a grey-haired, rugged-looking man with a red, bulbous nose and a white bushy beard that seemed to stop as it reached the top of his dark-blue jersey. He was sitting behind his desk in an untidy office, papers and charts scattered all over his desk, as well as all around the L-shape arrangement of tall filing cabinets behind him against the wall and round towards the window.

The office itself was a wooden building, shiplapped and tar black inside and outside with one large, square window facing out to the quay.

On the walls around the office more charts of the coast, maps of the local area as well as the Irish Sea and some showing the movement of the winds and tides all jostled and overlapped as they filled all the space like a quilted wallpaper. Along the wall facing the window there was a long cabinet of very narrow drawers in which were kept all the most up-to-date charts for the entire coastal regions of the UK and Western Europe.

Amongst the chaos in front of him, there was a bottle of rum and two glasses, much used and never washed. Standing before him patiently was O'Hare, a tall, squared-jawed man, with black, scraggy hair and still, dark, penetrating, brown eyes that seemed to see everything and that showed he had experienced a very hard life. He was well built and strong, wearing a dirty jersey, oil-stained trousers and flat cap. He wiped the last of the oil from his hands onto a dirty rag and spoke softly, with a thick Irish accent.

'The lads were thinking of setting off this weekend.'

'Aye, that should be fine,' the Harbour Master replied with the long, lifting lilt of the Devonshire man, adding, 'But you might have to make other arrangements soon.'

'Oh?'

The Harbour Master picked up a letter from his desk and showed it to O'Hare, but before he could take it, the Harbour Master dropped it to the table again as he continued.

'Madame Gilbert's lawyer's been in touch. Says she's sending a couple of, if you can believe it, a couple of young ladies round to have a look at the boat!'

O'Hare stifled a laugh as he replied.

'Women! Huh, what they know about boats?'

'Nothing. Don't you worry about them. Have O'Brian and O'Connor left yet?'

'Picked the truck up this morning, be back tonight,' O'Hare confirmed.

'Okay.' The Harbour Master glanced out of his window. 'You better give that Mary Conti a good going-over, especially along her bottom.'

'Right you are.' O'Hare raised his rag to the Harbour Master and then left, closing the door firmly behind him.

*

The brake drums bit with a dull squeal as the Riley came to a long, slow, gentle stop. Before them, the busy harbour was at work. Fish in their wooden trays and lobsters in their wicker baskets were being slung onto the quayside as young boys loaded the salted trays and dripping baskets onto the backs of the waiting open-back lorries which, when full, had their sides clipped back into place, and then trundled up the quayside, along the road and off to the nearby fish markets.

The engine died and after a second to let a lorry pass, Albert stepped out and around to the rear passenger door behind him. As he held it open, out stepped Samantha and Nicola in their light summer dresses and matching cloche hats.

'Thank you, Albert.' Samantha smiled, holding a hand

up to keep the sunlight from her eyes as she glanced around her until she saw the sign for the Harbour Master's office. 'We shouldn't be too long,' she added as Albert noticed that there was a public house just the other side of the harbour entrance.

'In that case, Miss, would you mind if I have a small drink whilst I wait?' He nodded slightly to the pub as he closed the car door.

'No. Ab-so-lute-ly,' she replied, adding, 'We might even join you afterwards. Could do with a glass of the old giggle water myself!'

'Very good, Miss.' He bowed slightly and watched as Samantha and Nicola made their way over to the office.

*

They knocked on the inner office door.

'Come in,' the Harbour Master called and Samantha and Nicola entered. They were surprised to find the room so untidy. The Harbour Master and another man were sitting either side of the desk, each drinking straight from a beer bottle they were sharing.

Seeing the two women, the Harbour Master quickly straightened himself up, hiding the bottle in a drawer in his desk as he stood.

'Morning, Miss,' he greeted her warmly. 'And what can I do you for?'

'Good morning.' Samantha smiled warmly, hiding her shock. 'I understand you have a boat here, which belongs to a friend of ours, whose husband sadly passed away and I'm here to inspect the vessel on her behalf. Her lawyer should have informed you.'

The Harbour Master thought for a moment.

'What? That French fellow's fluff?' He quickly cursed himself and corrected his language. 'I mean woman. Yes, right, Miss.'

'So, may we see it?' Samantha asked.

The Harbour Master moved a couple of papers off his desk to retrieve his hat and with a shrug to the other man he made his way around the desk.

'Suppose!' He pulled his Breton cap on and pushed past Samantha and Nicola who, aghast at his rudeness, followed him out.

9

The harbour was made of two walls, one that ran from the warehouses on the west side and stretched out into the sea the full width of the sheltered bay before making a dogleg back round, parallel with the land and for the full length of the bay, before it turned back towards land and came to an abrupt end, where a small lighthouse stood. The gap was wide enough for more than one boat to pass another at the mouth, no matter how bad its captain was, before the shorter wall, a virtually straight jetty ran back to shore.

The Harbour Master, Samantha and Nicola all stood on the quay looking out at a bay which was mostly all mud with smaller craft moored on posts on slack lines sitting rather unceremoniously on the thick, stinking, sticky, brown silt, whilst at the far harbour wall, where some water still remained, there were a couple of larger vessels moored, the largest of them an expensive steam yacht.

'There you are,' the Harbour Master announced, looking out with a pointed gaze at the far harbour wall.

They looked out beyond the small fishing boats but didn't know what they were looking for.

'Where?' Nicola asked.

'Out there!' He nodded in the boats' general direction as a gull's cry echoed overhead.

'Where out there?' Samantha asked. 'Which one's the Cœur d'Or?'

'The Cœur's the one with the big thing sticking out of the middle,' he replied unhelpfully as all the boats, but for the very small rowing boats, or fishing longboats had either a mast or a funnel sticking out the middle of them.

'You couldn't give me a small hint could you, only boats are not my thing really?' Samantha told him.

'Ship, ma'am.'

'I may be a novice, but all the same. My interest in is cars.'

'I mean out there.' He pointed to it. 'The big yacht, anchored out in the bay.'

'You mean the one with the red-and-black chimney?' Nicola asked helpfully noticing how it differed from the other one.

'Funnel,' he replied.

'Probably, but it is the one with the red and black chimney?' she asked again, giving him a placating smile.

'Aye. That's the one.' He sighed. He hated landlubbers. He wished they'd stay on the land and leave the sea to those who knew what it was all about.

'But, but, it's so big!' Samantha exclaimed, shielding her eyes from the sun as she stared at it, realising that this yacht was much bigger than she had anticipated.

'Should be!' The Harbour Master remarked flippantly. 'She was built in '22, for some Spanish Count who has a lot of business interests around Spain, Morocco, Monaco, Italy, and France. Imports, casinos, clubs that sort of thing,

I suspect he used it sailing around the Mediterranean watching over his empire. But I understand in '25 he sold it to Mr Gilbert so he could buy something a bit fancier.' Samantha nodded as she half listened, he continued. 'She's twin diesel, built of quarter-inch Norwegian steel plate 'lapped' and then riveted with 'speed' rivets.' He turned to the two women and continued in a condescending tone as he didn't expect them to understand anything too technical. 'Which means they're countersunk on the outside for a smooth hull surface.' He turned back to the boat as he continued. 'The decks are of two-inch teak, packed with cotton and caulked with a black rubber compound. Teak panels outside and walnut panelling inside fitted around the deck and wheel house. Below decks the yacht has three double staterooms and three single staterooms with three bathrooms. The raised panelling, below decks in the staterooms, are all painted ivory with walnut trim. Doors are walnut and there are walnut-panelled hallways and stairs.'

'Quite comfortable then?' Samantha asked with a slightly ironic tone. And it seemed quite lavish. Pierre loved the lavish and richly overstated. It was certainly the sort of yacht Pierre would have bought, she had to agree. He had always been the sort of man who liked to show off his wealth, even when he hadn't had any, but, she couldn't get out of her mind that this boat, or any boat, even a rowing boat, wasn't Pierre. He was loud, brash, a great racing driver, a woman's man, a cake-eater extraordinaire. But a sailor? She remembered he'd once commented he used to feel seasick walking over the Pont de l'Archevêché or though there could have been another reason for that as there was a nice bistro just facing the bridge on its south side they used to spend a lot of time in.

'I'd say,' the Harbour Master continued, 'and her mechanicals are of the finest and most modern construction. Her two fifty-inch bronze propellers turn 60 feet away from the two 300 horsepower Winton six-cylinder diesel engines via five-inch diameter cold-rolled, steel shafts. Electricity's produced by 7,500 watt generators driven by a six-cylinder petrol engine. The anchor, windlass, steering gear and refrigeration are all electrically operated.'

'So you don't need a crew down in the engine room to drive her?' Samantha asked.

'No,' the Harbour Master replied, continuing, 'but you will need someone to maintain her if you're planning on taking her out for a long voyage. The heating system is a steam boiler with radiators in all rooms and compartments. Drop-down plate glass windows in the salons and wheel house, along with electric fans below deck for ventilation.' He beamed with pride. 'All that and she's only 124 foot.'

'That's a lot bigger than I was expecting.' Samantha was impressed. 'We were of the opinion it would only be twenty or so feet long!'

'Aye, there you are. The Cœur's a mighty beast. Take you easily down to the Azores.'

'But there's no gangway. How do we get onto her?' she asked, turning to him.

'You need a dinghy, Miss.'

'I need a what?' Samantha replied.

'Or you could borrow my rowing-boat and row out to her.'

'Row?' she asked, as suddenly she began to appreciate just how far away it was moored.

'It's okay, Miss.' He turned to her. 'Mr Gilbert, used to hire a dinghy to get him on and off the boat, on account of him only sailing her twice a year.'

'I see!'

'So, can someone row us out there now?' Nicola asked.

'"fraid not, Miss. Low tide, you see. The shore part of the harbour's all mud. Can't row in mud. Have to wait till high tide.'

'When's that?' Samantha asked. Turning back to her,

he replied, 'Next is one, fifty-two this afternoon, or two, forty-three in the morning. So, either come back later, or come back tomorrow. Be here by three, seventeen tomorrow afternoon and I'll take you over myself.'

Samantha and Nicola looked at each other and sighed as they both realised this quick favour was going to take a lot longer than they had imagined.

'Suppose we'd better come back later. If not, would tomorrow be fine with you?' Samantha sighed.

'I'm here from eight so it's fine by me.' He shrugged.

'I was hoping to finish it all today, but if we come back this afternoon, we won't have enough time to play a round of golf and I so wanted to take you to the same place Daddy took me, the time we were here together. I suppose we could spend some time in town?'

'Not to worry,' Nicola replied, adding, 'It's such a lovely day. Why don't we go to the beach?'

'And how!' Samantha agreed. 'That's just the cat's meow!'

*

Back in his office, the Harbour Master found the man was still sitting there, still drinking having retrieved the beer bottle from the desk, and had been joined by O'Hare, who was now all grimy and dirty, wiping his hands on a rag as he stood by the desk.

'Just finished greasing the Mary Conti,' O'Hare informed him as the Harbour Master removed his hat and slung it onto the charts cabinet.

'Good.'

'And am I right in thinking, that there be a rather posh motor out there near the quay. Does that mean we have a buyer at last for the Admiral Joff?'

'As I keep telling you, O'Hare, no one wants to buy a wooden yacht anymore. No one wants sail. They only want steam.' The Harbour Master crossed to the table, uncovered his bottle of rum and poured himself a large tin mug full. 'No.' He took a large sip that seemed to relax his straining nerves as he continued. 'If you must know. They're here to look at the Cœur d'Or.'

'Froggy's not sold her already, has she?' O'Hare asked, a note of panic echoed in his question.

'No, those were Madame Gilbert's reps.'

'Good, 'cos we're still on schedule.'

'Right.' He took another sip from his tin mug.

'For a minute, when I saw that Riley...' O'Hare crossed himself casually. '...thought the froggy had already sold the boat!'

The Harbour Master quickly drained his mug.

'No such luck.' He placed his mug back down firmly on the desk. 'A couple of wildcat-looking flappers if you ask me. Trouble if there ever was, I expect. Nothing's ever come out well mixing women and boats. At least they're off my harbour for the rest of the day.'

'Oh? How?' O'Hare asked.

'Because it's just a 'cat's meow' day. They're going to 'cat's meow' spend it down the 'cat's meowing' beach.' The Harbour Master then poured himself another quarter mug of rum. The stress was getting to him and he was aware it was beginning to show. With a subtle glance, he watched O'Hare for a moment beginning to mull things over in his mind.

'And they need to stay away. Well, at least until after the weekend,' O'Hare muttered.

'True. Once they've inspected it, who knows! I think, Paddy, you ought to be thinking of finding some alternative arrangements.'

But as he drank the rum, its sweet intoxication was no longer strong enough to blur out the burden that weighed heavily on his shoulders and it was that burden that was filling him with dread.

10

Samantha and Nicola were at the beach, splashing about in the water, though not wading out too far. The water was too cold and there was a bit of a breeze coming off it onto the land. Surrounded by a golden bay of sand, on an otherwise secluded and deserted stretch of coast, they bent down to scoop the water up to throw at each other, giggling and laughing.

Earlier, on the clifftop, they had changed into their bathing suits with their little modesty skirts, stockings that came almost to the knee, beach shoes and swimming caps. Both costumes were dark blue with white piping.

A little way from the cliff and the wet sand, on the soft, fine sand, resting on a large travel rug, there were a couple of canvas bags in which they had their clothes and two large towels on top of a large, wicker food hamper.

The bay curved in from two outcrops making the

beach sheltered from the worst of any sea breeze, and the rolling waves coming around the outcrops showed how sheltered it was. They became quite sedate by the time they reached their beach. They were miles from any town, as the grass farmlands above stretched to the edge of the cliffs, and they were alone, but for a few sheep on the top. The pair were soon feeling all unrestrained, able to abandon their inhibitions.

They squealed and they laughed, joked and frolicked in the water, their laughter carrying around the tall rock and sandstone cliffs and for almost half an hour they enjoyed the warm sun and the cool salty water. Then as they began to tire, together, arm in arm, they went back up the beach, over the hard, wet sand and then onto the soft, ever-shifting, dry sand, over to their bags.

'Lovely spot. So secluded,' Nicola remarked as she gently set herself down on the travel rug.

'I think that's why Daddy brought the cottage.' Samantha knelt down beside her near to her bag. 'He usually stays in hotels.' She looked along the beach adding casually, 'but sometimes he likes to have a bit of peace and quiet for entertaining. Though the beach down in the bay, I understand, is just as lovely.'

'Though not so quiet.'

Samantha rummaged in her bag and took out her silver cigarette case, with the pink enamel inlay, and black holder. She offered the open cigarette case to Nicola, who took one, before taking one for herself. She snapped the case shut and tossed it back into her bag before placing her cigarette into the holder and then rummaging around inside her bag again to find her little matching silver lighter. Nicola leant back on her hand as she looked out over the sea, shielding her eyes from the sun with the hand holding the cigarette.

'Shall we have something to eat?' Samantha asked as she found the lighter. Then, she spun the wheel and the spark ignited the flame. She drew on the small Bakelite tube and the tip of her cigarette began to glow orange.

'Maybe we should,' Nicola replied as she took the lighter from Samantha. 'I need to get my strength back if I'm to get you back for dunking me earlier!'

'I'll just see what Albert made for us.' As Samantha unfastened the two leather straps of the hamper, Nicola lit her cigarette. She let the lid fall back to the rug, then as she peered in, Samantha smiled warmly to herself as she was happy to see that Albert, as usual, had well and truly exceeded her expectations.

'He's made us some cold ham sandwiches, some chicken drumsticks, scotch eggs and pork pies, some coleslaw, potato salad, some Dundee cake and a couple of bottles of ginger beer. And we've some milk, tea, a kettle and small tea pot and I think that must be the bottle of meths for the primus.'

'He certainly knows how to look after us!' Nicola agreed.

'Maybe we should do something for him tonight?'

Samantha took out the small primus stove and placed it down on the centre of the rug before turning back to the hamper to pull out the two stoneware bottles of ginger beer.

'Like what?' Nicola asked, completely perplexed. 'What could two young birds like us possibly do for him?'

'You're so right.' Samantha sighed disappointedly. 'What can two young birds like us, together, do for such a man! It's not like I'm a great cook or anything. That's one of the things they didn't teach us at school. Apparently they had a special school for that!'

She handed Nicola her ginger beer before pulling the stopper out of her own and taking a quick refreshing sip of the warm, spicy, sugary drink.

'Does he have any hobbies?' Nicola asked as she toyed with the stopper of her bottle.

'He does like unusual things.' Samantha agreed. 'Maybe we could find him an unusual shell or something?'

'What here?' Nicola asked. 'On the beach?'

'Yes.' Samantha pushed the stopper back into her bottle as she placed it down on the sand beside her.

'And how.' Nicola smiled. 'I saw some earlier near the cliff as we approached.'

'Atta girl!' Samantha quickly glanced over to the slope in the cliff, the only way down onto the beach. 'Why don't you quickly have a look and see if there is anything really good over there? After all, you're the one with the keen eye.'

Nicola smiled again, embarrassed a little by her flattery.

'Okay.'

'Whilst you do that, I'll sort out our lunch,' Samantha added as she shuffled closer to the hamper so she could reach the lid, where the plates and cutlery were fastened.

She watched as Nicola rose and walked over to the cliff to a number of shells lying at random in a wave-washed pile at the foot of rocky outcrop.

In the lid of the hamper, fastened in a cross-pattern of straps, were the enamel plates, with the cutlery between them. As Nicola began to root around amongst the pile of shells at the cliff-face, Samantha unfastened the straps to the larger set of plates, taking two of them, and placed them next to her on the rug, before she took out the first of the Bakelite tubs from which she spooned out some potato salad onto each plate.

She looked up and smiled contently to herself with the gentle warmth of affection as she watched the girl of her dreams, oblivious to her, collecting some shells from the sand.

She found it charming the way Nicola would push the seaweed or the stones and other shells away with the tip of her shoe before suddenly, like a heron spearing a fish, dart down, picking up a shell, before searching for another, disregarding the odd occasional old one for a newer one each time, in her hunt for the perfect shell. Watching her gentle soft frame, so slender, with her brown hair poking out around the bottom of her swimming cap, it was like the innocent child had been reborn, a joy in all things rekindled.

It warmed her heart, making her feel all goofy, to see Nicola enjoying herself, so relaxed and happy in the sun, that she couldn't help but feel a pride she didn't want to share with anyone else, that she almost forgot about getting ready their picnic.

Samantha unfastened the knives and forks to place by the plates on the rug, before picking up her own canvas bag, untying it quickly and taking from it her brand new Leica A. Quickly she slipped off the lens cap, leaving it dangling by its cord, raised the viewing window and pulled the lens out ready.

It was a 35mm camera. She liked the format as it was the same she'd used making movies, only this time the film was fed horizontally past the 50mm lens, the preferred prime lens used in the movies which meant, even without a rangefinder, her years of experience both in front of and behind the camera enabled her to bring any subject into sharp focus without the aid of a measuring tape, something she found difficult on the occasions when she'd used a box Brownie.

She'd ordered it before Porky had talked her into racing again at the Mille Miglia, his grand idea of her making a comeback, though, thanks to the crash and then radiator trouble twenty miles from the line, they'd only come eighth, probably her worst result since her first early days.

Her fee for the race had been one hundred dollars and this camera had been ordered from Germany. She'd worked out, given the current exchange rate; it had cost her eighty-eight dollars, and £1,6s,6d in postage.

What frightened her about the purchase wasn't so much the cost, but the realisation she could spend so much without thinking about it. Her personal manager at the building society had told her withdrawing such an amount wouldn't affect her base capital as it was less than she'd had earned that year in interest and so, why not.

The Leica folded flat and had no cardboard or canvas parts, just right for an enthusiastic photographer out and about, though the specifications were sparse. Shutter speeds from the cloth, focal-plane shutter covered 1/25 - 1/500 second. The lens couldn't be detached and the viewfinder was mounted separately on the top plate. It was a good camera, with a wonderful Leitz Anastigmat lens, was lightweight and fitted well in her hand. She just loved the vulcanite body with its leather pattern effect.

She checked her shutter speed and looked up at the sky to make sure she was right, before she sat down, keeping one foot flat in the sand so that she could rest her elbow into the crease between calf muscle and thigh and, with her hand holding the camera base, she watched Nicola in the frame window, her other hand with index finger poised on the button, as she waited until she was still.

She pressed the button, there was a crisp snap sound and then Nicola poking around with her toe at some more seaweed was captured forever. She rolled the film on with the wheel next to the viewfinder and when it stopped, locked and loaded ready, she made herself ready once more, capturing Nicola in her frame again.

*

Up high on the cliffs, a shadowy figure moved to the edge.

*

There was an assortment of white shells at her feet, some large, some small. Some broke easily as she stepped upon them, but she didn't notice as she stared intently at them all, looking for that illusive special one. Then, as she kicked away with the toe of her swimming shoe some old black seaweed that was covering some shells and a small outcrop of rock, there it was, a large flat white shell, with a pearl-like yellow sheen, a swirling marble pattern rippling through it.

Quickly she bent down to pick it up and as she held it aloft into the light, she could see the lustre and sheen of the highly polished surface twinkle in the sunlight.

'What do you think of this one?' she called back to Samantha, holding it out towards her.

'Let me see?'

Then, as Nicola started back to Samantha, there was a crashing thud and the thin echo of splitting shells as a large stone gargoyle fell inches behind her to rest partly buried in the soft yellow sand by the force of its fall.

She looked back startled, then up at the cliff as, equally startled, Samantha, placing her camera down on the rug, rushed over to her and came to her side, putting an arm around her, to comfort her more for her own sake as she was shaking, while Nicola, more bemused than troubled, looked up at the cliff edge.

*

High on the cliff, the shadowy figure silently slipped back through the long grass, away from the bay.

*

Still in each other's embrace, they both looked at the gargoyle and then up at the clifftop.

'That could have killed me!' Nicola exclaimed, her voice trembling slightly. Then sudden panic and fear gripped her, as an ice chill ran down her spine.

'Strange,' Samantha mused as she noticed the rather monastic look of the lump of stone. 'I don't remember there being a church up there?'

'Not surprised if it keeps dropping onto the beach like that!!'

'Come back to the picnic. I'll pour you a ginger beer,' Samantha encouraged her, leading her to the rug.

Together, with Samantha still comforting Nicola, holding her gently with her arms around her, they made their way back to the travel rug and their waiting picnic.

11

Samantha and Nicola had a couple of fun hours at the beach before Albert returned with the Riley from his mid-morning break at the pub. It took them twenty minutes to pack up, and another twenty to drive back to town, arriving back at the harbour just after half one. They parked near to the Harbour Master's office and Albert opened the door facing the office to let Nicola and Samantha out.

'Thank you, Albert.' Samantha acknowledged him as he closed the door behind her.

'Miss.' He bowed, his body a little more loose than usual because he was beginning to feel a little tired. As Samantha and Nicola entered the building, he climbed back into the driver's seat, almost falling into it. He let the door swing shut, closed his eyes and was soon fast asleep.

*

The Harbour Master rowed Samantha and Nicola out to the Cœur d'Or.

'She's much bigger than she looked from the quay,' Samantha remarked, regretting it the moment she'd spoken.

'Would be. We're much closer,' he replied with a condescending tone.

Samantha sighed, frustrated partly that she had made herself seem a little dumb, but partly that he had misunderstood her. 'I meant, she looked so sleek and low. It's not until you get up close you realise just how like an iceberg she is, but in reverse.'

They came alongside the yacht where there were some rope steps and, after the Harbour Master had secured the boat to the mooring line, one by one, they stepped up the wooden planking between the ropes and on to the boat's lower deck.

As the Harbour Master joined Samantha and Nicola, they looked along the yacht.

'Of course, if you were thinking of entertaining, Miss,' he began, like the salesman he naturally was, 'I can have her brought in to harbour so your guests could board via the gangway. She's not difficult to crew. Including the stewards, you could probably get away with eight.'

'Thank you.' Samantha smiled sweetly. 'Shall we take a look around?'

'Thought we'd start at the bridge and make our way down,' he suggested, pointing the way, before adding as if it was an afterthought, 'You don't want to see the engines, do you, Miss?'

'Why not?' Samantha shrugged. 'I must report everything to Mrs Gilbert.'

'Right you are.' He touched the peak of his Breton cap and then, pointing past them, he said, 'This way. And be careful. The steps to the bridge are steep.' They followed him heading towards the front of the yacht.

*

The door slid open and the Harbour Master led them onto the bridge. It was a long, walnut-panelled room with large windows around the main three walls, with a similar sliding door at the far end to where the other side of the narrow deck led back to the upper deck.

In the centre, near the forward windows there was the large, traditional ship's wheel, made of mahogany and composed of eight cylindrical wooden spokes, each shaped like balusters and all joined at a central wooden nave covered by a brass nave plate, housing the axle which ran through a pedestal at waist height.

Between the wheel and the forward windows, sat the binnacle, a waist-high stand in which were all the navigational instruments, placed for quick and easy reference. On top was the yacht's magnetic compass, mounted in gimbals to keep it level as the yacht pitched and rolled at sea.

Next to the helm's position, left of the wheel but in easy reach, there was the chadburn, a communications device used to order engineers in the engine room to power the vessel at a required speed as indicated by the display on a dial that was on the side facing towards the wheel. The dial itself was about nine inches in diameter with a set of twin handles, a knob at the centre, and attached to an indicator pointer on the face of the dial. Under it there was also the revolutions per minute indicator, worked by a hand crank.

Originally, when the helm wanted to change speed, he would 'ring' the chadburn by moving the handle to a different position on the dial. This would ring a bell in the engine room and move their pointer to the position on the dial selected by the bridge. The engineers hearing the bell would move their handle to the same position to signal their acknowledgment of the order and adjust the engine speed accordingly. However, on this chadburn most of it was for decoration, to make it seem familiar to any real sailor as only the twin levers moved to drive each engine directly, the system being fully automatic.

It was made of brass, to look older and more sturdy, but the handle was covered by a mahogany sleeve to make it blend in with the wheel. On the wall, next to the binnacle, there were the voice pipes, four of them, to allow the bridge to communicate with key areas of the yacht.

Behind this narrow room there was a small passageway, with steps leading down into the yacht and next to them there was a small ante-room, the navigator's station in which all the charts and navigational equipment were kept.

The Harbour Master waited while they took a good look around the bridge and, when both women moved to the forward windows, overlooking the yacht's bow, he remarked, 'As you can see, all round visibility from the highest point on the ship and by the wheel all the controls you need to sail her. So, when you give a command up here, you don't have to wait for anyone down below to carry it out for you.'

'But she's still tiller driven?' Nicola asked, turning back to him. 'You turn opposite to the direction you want to go?' She could see he was a little taken aback, as if he hadn't expected either of them to know anything about boats and she noted he gave her a new begrudging respect as he replied.

'Oh yes. I know there's this new-fangled idea of rudder steering, but I don't think it will ever catch on. Anyway, this beauty was built in '24, so she's modern but with a hint of class. You want to see the cabins next?'

'Ab-so-lute-ly,' Samantha agreed.

'Then we'll start with the double staterooms.'

He opened the second sliding door and led them off the bridge.

As they began to walk back to the upper deck, Samantha turned to Nicola.

'Fancy you knowing so much about boats! I would never have thought it.'

'One of the many reasons why I decided to come to London,' Nicola explained, 'was that my father insist I went out with someone of rank in the Navy, the son of a friend of his from medical school. I think he thought he would be able to instil a bit of discipline into me and, of course, he thought that maybe we'd fall in love and marry.'

'So he had a rank. What was he? A Petty Officer?'

'Very,' Nicola agreed. 'The slightest thing would upset him terribly and I just knew I had to get away, if only for his own good, as I was very nearly in danger of bruising his fists.' She rubbed her shoulder, the bruising memory still smarting, as they in turn made their way down to the lower main deck. 'I'm not sure he liked the idea of me having a career. He wanted me to give up my work and start a family. Fortunately, we parted before I became a fecund little gooseberry bush, or else I'm not sure I would have ever been able to get away from him.'

*

The Harbour Master held the door open as Samantha and Nicola entered, coming in from entrance next to the bar, from the lower decks.

'And finally, the lounge, where you entertain people when the ship's at sea.'

'Very nice,' Samantha replied. Nicola crossed over to the piano and looked at it as Samantha sat in a comfortable chair.

The raised panelling in the lounge was all walnut with ivory inlays, making the room seem bright and airy, and more hotel than boat-like in all but the smallest of details. The entrance doors were walnut, matching the walnut-panelled hallways and stairs. At the far end, there was a mahogany bar, behind which, on the mirrored shelves sat the multicoloured bottles of bitters and spirits. Beneath them, stacked on their rims on special shelves, was a great array of crystal cocktail glasses.

To the left as they entered, there was an ebony-coloured piano near the bar, and the rest of the lounge had around the sides wrap-around sofas, tables and some single, round, tub chairs, all ivory in colour with dark-chocolate piping and very bright compared to the wooden decoration. The seating's positioning gave a good view through the wide rectangular windows. There was a deep red-and-white, art-deco patterned carpet that ran throughout, matching the colour of the shades of the clam-style uplighters and giving the lounge a real home from home feel.

'So you've seen over the whole boat. What do you want to do now, Miss?' the Harbour Master asked as Samantha felt the luxurious padding of the arms of her chair.

'She's a lovely craft. Good lines and so well maintained.' She had to admit, if this was all Pierre's style of choice, she had considerably misjudged his taste. She was an exquisite yacht, a prime example of the craft.

'As good as the day she rolled down the slipway,' he replied.

'And how,' she agreed. 'She's darb!'

'So, Miss?' he asked, glancing through a window to look back at the harbour as if he was anxious to leave. He rubbed the back of his left hand, as though he was itching to glance at his watch but stifling his urge to do so.

'Suppose the next thing to do....' Samantha was distracted as Nicola pressed a few keys that messed tunelessly together and turned to look at her. Nicola, realising the other two were looking at her, stopped and gave an apologetic shrug as she lowered the lid, before she crossed from the piano and headed over to the bar.

'Suppose I should give Mrs Gilbert a call and find out

what she wants me to do with it,' Samantha replied.

'Very good, Miss,' he agreed.

'She's a very lovely craft. Don't you agree, Nicky?'

Nicola turned from the assortment of bottles she was gazing at. 'And how. This bar back here is fully stocked.'

Samantha swung round in her seat. 'Is it really?'

'Ab-so-lute-ly.' Nicola beamed as Samantha crossed over to her while the harbour master sighed in frustration.

'Copacetic. That's just swell!' Samantha exclaimed. 'Have they a cocktail list behind there?'

Nicola checked under the counter, feeling along the shelf. The Harbour Master rubbed the back of his hand again as he looked out towards the harbour.

'Miss. I do think we should be going?' the Harbour Master reminded her, pointing out to sea.

'Don't really want to be a wet blanket but we should get back to shore and call Sylvie,' Samantha reluctantly admitted, leaning on the bar with one hand

'And how.' Nicola agreed, still not having found the cocktail book.

'We're in no hurry, baby. She's not going anywhere. We can come back sometime later and have a cocktail. What do you think?' Nicola smiled wickedly as Samantha added, 'And we could also give one of those staterooms a try, find out if she's comfortable for a long voyage. Might even be an idea to test the engines, take her out in the water. I mean, if Pierre did only use her a couple of times a year, then we'll have to make sure she's up to a long crossing.'

The Harbour Master paled slightly but didn't let them see.

'Test her engines? A long crossing?' he asked.

'Ab-so-lute-ly,' Samantha replied. 'In case Mrs Gilbert wants to sell her over in France. A lovely yacht like this would be just the bees' knees down in Cannes at high season.'

He hated landlubbers, as already they were beginning

to meddle with his plans.

12

Albert had woken with a start, as some gulls had sat on the car's bonnet, crying away, and that, and the dull, tinny chimes of the ropes rattling against their masts had made him feel guilty, reminding him of the seconds ticking away. A look at his watch had told him Miss Bishop had been gone for half an hour and with a glance over to the yacht he could see that the dinghy was still tied to the mooring line and, as it was such a large yacht, she was bound to be away for some time yet, so he resolved to do something useful with his time.

He took a bucket from a pile of them around the back of the Harbour Master's office, and at a nearby standpipe he was able to fill it with water. Taking an old rag from the boot and with his jacket and hat left on the front passenger seat, he quickly set about washing the car down. He took his time to get into all the small nooks and crannies, fearing that the salt in the air couldn't be good for the long-term health of the car's metal parts, but it wasn't long before the little Riley was cleaned.

The breeze was stiffening as it was now coming off the sea. Albert, with his chamois leather and tin of wax polish which he kept in the front passenger door pocket, carefully wiped away the clouds of white wax from the bonnet, until it began to glisten as if newly painted with a shimmering, still, water-like glaze.

All done, as he stepped wearily backwards to admire his work, wiping away the sweat from his brow, a gull swooped down, flying over the car, and dropped a long, white line of crap across the bonnet. He sighed with frustration and cursed the bird under his breath before dipping his old rag into his bucket of water and starting to wipe the mess away.

*

In the Harbour Master's office, Samantha perched on the edge of the desk, her legs crossed, holding the candlestick phone in both hands, waiting for the operator as she depressed the rockers once more.

The Harbour Master was sitting behind his desk, puffing on his rosewood pipe as Nicola, sitting in the other chair, leant against the desk next to Samantha so she could hear the conversation. She gazed at her smooth, alabaster neck, and glanced adoringly at Samantha's long slender legs in her thin, white-silk stockings, which brought a little smile to her lips as Samantha tapped her foot in the air to an imaginary beat.

'Paris 42, 42.' Samantha asked the operator and then waited while she was connected. 'Good afternoon. May I speak to Madame Gilbert, please?' She stopped tapping her foot, as she waited for Sylvie to take the phone. It seemed to take a long time and she suspected Sylvie had been in the conservatory enjoying a cup of coffee and reading as that was the downstairs room furthest from the phone. 'Sylvie, it's Samantha. Yes, I'm well. Nicky's just swell. Baby, I've just been looking over your yacht. She's a lovely craft, the cat's meow, darling.'

She waited as Sylvie replied, but Nicola couldn't hear what was said. Just then, Samantha glanced over to her and gave her a little sexy wink, which made Nicola blush ever so slightly. She took her compact out of her handbag and touched up her makeup so that the Harbour Master wouldn't notice.

'Maybe,' Samantha continued, 'but, as you know, with all that beating one's gums from across the pond, it's not really a good time to sell to people here. Maybe if you could get it to France, you might be able to find a buyer there? I mean, baby, all those rich Yankees. But over here, it could be a number of weeks.'

*

With his ear pressed to the office door, O'Hare listened intently as he faintly heard Samantha continue.

'Oh yes, she's seaworthy. Be a gas. We could take her down to the Riviera for you if you like?'

He was suddenly gripped by an icy cold fear as he then heard her say, 'Cannes? Swell!'

*

'I see.' She held the mouthpiece to her chest and turned to Nicola, noticing she was looking rather bemused. 'She has family down that way. They can handle it for her. Be the berries.'

'And how!' Nicola exclaimed.

'Okay, we'll arrange that from this end. If you need to contact me before then, we're staying at Daddy's seaside cottage. That's Torquay 34, 43. Bye.' She then replaced the earpiece and set the phone down again on the desk as she slipped from the corner and picked up her handbag.

'So?' Nicola asked as she leant back in her chair.

'Looks like we'll be sailing her down to Cannes. I'll get Albert to sort out some provisions and if we need any extra crew, we can hire your fellows here. Isn't that right?' she asked the Harbour Master.

'Yes, Miss.' He replied without taking the pipe from his mouth.

Samantha looked at her watch.

'Good. I'm so glad.' She tapped the glass and smiled. 'I think we can go into town, buy up some charts before dinner, and play the short course today. Then we'll have all tomorrow to play a round and let Albert make all the other arrangements whilst we're on the links.'

'And how,' Nicola agreed. 'I told you it wasn't a waste to leave the beach so early.'

They held eye contact for a moment, as a soft, warm ripple coursed through Samantha's veins. She felt as if she was full of fire and just wanted to kiss Nicola, there and then, that twinkle in Nicola's eyes setting her heart racing, but then she remembered where they were and became aware that the Harbour Master might notice the silence.

'I think a quick trip to the Lyons Tea Rooms and have ourselves some refreshments first? Does that sound the bees knees?'

Nicola smiled, that twinkle still sparkling brightly.

'Ab-so-lute-ly.'

13

Despite the bright sunlight trying to stream in through the etched window peeking through the gap between the loosely drawn, red-velvet curtains that hung on their loose, brass rings on the scuffed and stained brass rail across the entrance, the saloon bar was a dingy, musty place.

Its floors were covered in small piles of sawdust, and, like all the other buildings on the quayside, it had black, tar-stained walls and a blood-red, mahogany bar top, with a couple of firkins resting at the wall end and two sets of four taps separated by a bar towel around the middle of its length. The room was virtually bare of furniture, but even the small number of pedestal tables set sparsely around the room created a feeling of claustrophobia. Halfway along the bar that faced the entrance doors, there was a screen closing off the lounge bar, a thick oak panel with small glass windows along the top, just taller than a man, each with the brewery's logo, like the dirty etched window that looked out onto the quay, scored upon their surface.

In a corner, near an etched-glass window, which bathed them in sunlight, standing around one such pedestal table were O'Hare with O'Brian, a smaller man with round glasses and a thinning top of black hair, O'Keefe, a tall, thin man, with a hard-looking face and short, cropped, blond hair and O'Connor, a man of average height, with short, brown hair and a small scar under his left eye, which, with his stubbly chin, gave him an air of menace. Each of them was dressed like O'Hare as they all worked in the harbour and each had a stout and a cigarette, which they puffed on intently.

'Glad you could all make it, boys.' O'Hare spoke first, raising his glass, 'Ourselves alone,' then taking a sip of his stout.

'Anything for the cause,' O'Connor replied surreptitiously, as he and the others raised their glasses before having a sip, so that no one watching would know it was a toast.

'Well, we have bad news, boys,' O'Hare continued as they listened carefully. 'Those two English women sent down to look over the Cœur d'Or, I overheard them talking with Mrs Gilbert on the telephone. They intend to take the boat down to the south of France.'

'Nice, the south of France!' O'Brian exclaimed, dragging on his cigarette.

'That's what I heard.'

'Only I saw them earlier, so I did, when I was coming back from the Lisa Brie Two,' O'Connor continued. 'Pretty pair, looked like a couple of those flapper types, you know, like we saw in that film the other day with that Louise Brooks.'

'What were you doing on the Lisa Brie Two?' asked O'Keefe.

'Only painting the keel. You know, the eejit had only

gone and grounded her on a sandbank along the Solent. I mean really, the eejit.'

'I saw that film with Louise Brooks. She was gorgeous,' replied O'Brian. 'You being a married man and all!'

O'Connor blushed.

'I preferred that one with Harold Lloyd. You remember. When he was the rich boy who ended up on a pirate ship crewed only by all those really gorgeous women,' O'Brian continued. 'Though you could tell none of those women had ever been in a boat, never mind gone to sea.'

'Don't think they were there for their sailing skills,' O'Connor replied with a gleeful grin.

'And you a married man and all.' O'Brian sighed. 'And you say, those English were like... flappers too?'

O'Hare slapped the table hard.

'I don't care what they are!' O'Hare sighed, frustrated, as he clenched his fist. 'That's not the point.' He took a long welcome sip of his drink to calm himself down as his pals watched. He beckoned them closer to him so that they couldn't be overheard. 'We've another shipment just arrived from Spain and we need to ship it over to Cork by the weekend. We can't do that, whilst those nosy-parker flappers, or whatever you want to call them, are poking their noses into everything.'

'So what do you suggest?' asked O'Brian

'We take them out.'

'Can't do that!' O'Connor interrupted. 'I'm a happily married man.'

'I meant, we bump them off!' O'Hare sighed as O'Connor replied with an understanding nod.

'But they're just a couple of women!' O'Brian reminded them.

'Are you committed to the cause?' O'Hare quickly rounded on him. Feeling awkward and a little intimidated, O'Brian replied.

'Aye. But they're just a couple of women.'

'Just a couple of women, heh.' O'Hare rolled his eyes skyward as if he couldn't believe what he was hearing, as if he had just been cut to the quick. 'Just a couple of women. You pansies make me sick. Have you men no stomach for the task?' He glanced at each one of them in turn and in turn, they turned away to avoid his gaze. 'I was with Liam Lynch from the start,' he hissed under his breath, the anger still raw. 'I fought the Black and Tans in '21. I fought with his boys in Kerry and I was interned in Kilmainham Gaol with Eamon de Valera back in '24, so don't for one moment think I'm not committed to the cause.' O'Hare slammed the table defiantly with his clenched fist before continuing. 'There should be no treaty.' The regret hung heavy in every word. 'Collins sold us out to be a puppet of the imperial British. We are the army of the republic, boys, and all traitors of the cause and all those who support the 'Free State' and the partition of our birthright must suffer the fate of those like Kevin O'Higgins for their crimes against the Irish People.'

'Well, when you put it like that!' O'Brian shrugged empathically.

'So you're with me, comrades?' O'Hare asked, looking each square in the eye.

They look at each other around the table and nodded.

'When?' O'Keefe asked.

'We need to get the goods on the boat over the next two nights, so I suggest we do it this afternoon,' O'Hare answered and then took a sip of his drink.

'Okay. But do we know where they're going to be?' O'Brian asked still a little uneasy about where the events were leading.

'No, but I know where they are now,' O'Hare replied.

'Where would that be, then?' O'Brian asked.

'The Lyon's Tea Rooms in town.'

'We can't do anything there! There be too many people and, besides, my sister's best friend's cousin works there.'

O'Hare dragged heavily upon his cigarette. 'Then I heard the 'La-di-da' one say they were going to play a round of golf.'

'And where would that be I wonder?' O'Brian asked.

'At the golf course?' O'Connor suggested sarcastically.

'But which one?' O'Brian asked. 'There are so many around here!'

O'Hare smiled. 'That's why, fellers, I suggest we head down to the tea room and find out where they're going. We'll plan what to do then.'

Then, as one, they took a sip of their stouts.

14

The Lyons Tea Room was on the corner of two streets, giving it two walls of window with a perfect view of the bustling high street and main street, where the busy crowd filtered between the cars and carts as they jostled past one another.

The small, square tables were positioned in neat rows with seating for two or four around them as required. The nippies in their black dresses with the double row of buttons, white aprons and white maid's hats flittered like wisps from customer to customer, taking orders and bringing them their teas, fast and efficiently, with the kindness, grace and a smile which made their tea rooms superior to any in the world.

Samantha and Nicola were sitting at a table for two near the window, with a pot for two and a two-tier cake stand laden with fancy cream and iced cakes, which they were enjoying. Behind them, dressed in their finest Sunday best, even though it was still quite shabby by the standards of the rest of the customers there, O'Hare and O'Connor entered, with their hair washed and brushed back and their hands cleaned, even right down to their fingernails, looking almost middle class.

They were met by one of the Lyons waitresses and shown to a table not too far away from Samantha and Nicola's, just in earshot, despite the mumbling hum of the other customers and noises from the kitchen.

'Nice relaxing cup of tea in such civilised surroundings,' Samantha noted as behind them, O'Hare and O'Connor gave their order to a waitress.

'And how,' Nicola agreed, looking over the French fancies on the top tier.

'And the view's pretty nice too.' Nicola wasn't so sure she preferred a busy street to the tranquillity of the beach but Samantha added with a devilish grin, 'All these waitresses in their little white aprons.'

Nicola shook her head slightly and, with teasing disbelief, asked, 'You're not keen, are you?'

'How could I be with anyone else when I have you?'

They held hands briefly as they smiled to each other. Then, aware someone might see, they both took cakes off the stand, placed them on their plates and began to eat them with cake forks.

'Do you think it will take us long to sail round to the south of France?' Samantha asked and then took a quick sip of her tea. Nicola began to calculate in her mind the distance taking into account what she knew about the yacht's performance and what she could remember about the tides and currents she'd been told by the sailors her father had treated when he'd been called down to the docks.

Behind them, the waitress returned with two plates. On one there was eggs on toast which she placed down in front of O'Hare, the other a Welsh rabbit she placed before O'Connor. The waitress then smiled, saying she hoped they would enjoy their meal as she left them.

'Would depend on our average speed,' Nicola began as she cradled her cup of tea in her hands and then took a sip, while O'Connor took a longing look at what O'Hare had on his plate. 'But say we could keep her at 8 knots, that's just over 9 miles an hour as a nautical mile is just over 2026 yards, longer than a land mile which is 1760 yards.' Nicola began to quickly tot up the total in her mind as she hovered the cup ready to take yet another sip, but didn't. Behind her, after a moment looking at O'Hare's plate and standing slightly, O'Connor leant across the table, fork in hand, trying to help himself to a piece of O'Hare's egg.

Instinctively, O'Hare quickly put his arm around his plate to protect it and O'Connor dejectedly sat down to get comfortable again. 'So that's a maximum of 192 miles a day, but it could be less, as there are currents and winds which, even though we're not under sail, would still have a bearing on the speed we could reach,' Nicola continued. O'Connor pulled the table slightly closer to him, making O'Hare's protecting arm knock his plate off and onto his lap. Nicola sighed and shrugged slightly. 'To have a more definite figure I would need to see the charts for the areas, but….'

Nicola took a sip of her tea as, much to his displeasure, O'Hare picked up his plate, then his eggs and toast, which he unceremoniously dumped back onto his plate and as he stood, the soggy stain on his lap still dripped with the grease from the eggs. 'I'd say to be safe….' She put her cup back down on her saucer. 'We would cover only 150 miles a day and we'd have to sail past Spain, Portugal, and Gibraltar before we reach France.' O'Hare slapped O'Connor across the head, then as he sat down again, the two of them continued to eat their lunch.

'You see those birds on the next table?' Nicola asked,

slyly indicating to O'Hare and O'Connor.

'The bunny's making off-time jive?' Samantha asked glancing quickly in their direction.

'Don't they work at the docks? Well, one does I'm sure, didn't we see him working on that yacht in dry dock, scrapping by the keel.'

'The what?'

'The long fin thing that keeps it stable in the water.' Nicola explained.

'Level with me, what's the beef?'

'Don't you think it's a bit odd, them being here and not down the pub I mean?'

'Don't razz, or they'll think you're on a blue nozzle curse, maybe that's why they've got the heebie-jeebies, they're just a pair of palookas', living like an egg. It's none of our beeswax really. I'd say half the town at least visits this Lyons corner house at least once a week, they're very popular, swell service, swanky looking and at a price you don't need no sap for his dough. If it wasn't for the room being full of tomatoes, they wouldn't stand out like a couple of lollygagger's come in from the cold.'

'And how, I can be all wet at times.'

'Baloney, now forget those birds, what were you saying?'

Nicola summed up. 'I'd allow us three weeks and we'd have to pull into harbour a couple of times on the way to re-fuel.'

'So we're going to need to pack a few trunks. No way am I wearing the same cocktail dress more than once in a week!' Samantha commented as she poured some more hot water into the teapot. 'Shall I ask for some more hot water?' She turned, about to call over a waitress.

'No, thank you.' Nicola stopped her. 'I think six cups is enough! And anyway, shouldn't we be heading off soon? If you want to play a round, we're going to need to get out of these clothes first.'

'Baby, you're right,' Samantha agreed. 'Even as

visitors they won't let us on the greens if we're not properly dressed. We'll just finish this pot then we'll cut along.'

15

The Riley gently pulled to a wailing stop, as the two drum brakes bit and the car slowly slid across the blue-grey gravel drive to come to rest between two other parked cars. Albert adjusted his cap and then stepped out, closing his door behind him before opening and stepping back with the door in hand to let Samantha and Nicola climb out.

They were both dressed in short white skirts, with matching stockings and shoes, and both had a jumper and a large, baggy flat cap. As they stood waiting, Albert went round to the back of the car, opened the box and took from it two sets of golf clubs, each in a brown leather golfing bag and their brown golf shoes, their studs newly tightened and ready.

'Your clubs, Miss.' He handed one set of clubs and shoes to Samantha and as he handed Nicola hers he added,

'Miss.' Nicola slung her bag over her shoulder. 'I've already taken care of your temporary memberships, Miss, and you're up at five.'

'Very good, Albert,' Samantha replied. 'What are you going to do whilst we're playing?'

'Thought I might spend my time in the visitors bar, might read a newspaper, catch up on the local gossip. That sort of thing, Miss.'

'Very good. We'll see you at six.'

'Very good, Miss,' he replied and watched as they both headed into the clubhouse.

It was a tall, grand, grey house that at one time had been a Georgian industrialist's country mansion and Albert could imagine the likes of Mr Darcy and Jane Eyre living there, or was it Jane Austen or Jane Biggleswade? Was it Darcy or Rochester? He couldn't remember. It had been such a long time since he'd read the book and one story about Georgian morals was pretty much like another. However, what he could remember was these houses were big and had high ceilings and were very plush inside. Though this was no longer a home, the rooms devoted now to offices and conference rooms and whatever else was needed for the members to run a high-class golf course, he could still let his imagination transport him back to a time when everyone went around by horse and cart and there were no bonnets to be mess on by the gulls.

Once both the flappers were out of sight, he relaxed. He was again off duty with no chores to do, so without any further hesitation, he made his way around the grand house to a side door. But little did he know that, from the bushes by the entranceway, O'Keefe and O'Brian watched.

*

They had reached the green on the third. Nicola was holding the flag out of the hole as Samantha stood a couple of yards away, putter in hand and her bag of clubs lying on the grass off the green, carefully judging the ball and her soft swing three times while eyeing the distance to the cup.

Samantha enjoyed the game even though she thought herself not very good at it. For her it was something relaxing, an excuse to get out and walk. She'd picked the habit up in Los Angeles, as no one walked there. She had tried once to walk from her rented house to go just around the block, and it had taken her six hours, two of which had been down at the West Hollywood police precinct when some resident had reported her as a vagrant. After the studio had assured them she wasn't, she had then had to spend most of that time signing autographs and having her pictures taken with the officers.

Golf was the only way 'the-well-to-do' did any walking in Hollywood. Even the beach was really only a place to sit by the sea and pose, a place to be seen, and as she'd always been a girl who liked to be out and about rather than sitting indoors, reading a paper whilst listening to the radio or gramophone, she'd made the step and allowed herself to join in with a set who would spend all their spare time playing the game.

It was where her next role in her next picture was discussed, where she met her leading men after she'd shot the screen test and it had also been where most the party invites had come from.

Playing the game for two years twice a week, well, she might not have been up to a professional standard, but she certainly wasn't as bad as your average amateur.

She held her breath and eased her stroke though the ball. It gently trundled down the green to the hole's edge and dropped in with nice crisp clatter.

She retrieved her ball before putting her putter back in her bag and making a note on her card. Samantha took the flag from Nicola, who she saw was looking a little hesitant. She watched as Nicola crossed to her bag, almost at the edge of the green next to where her ball sat.

Nicola gripped the club in her hands and stood with her legs apart. That bit she understood, but as she looked at where the ball was and then where the hole was. What was supposed to happen next was a mystery. She knew there were a few yards the ball had to travel and in a straight line, but how this worked, how it was some people could hit it straight and for some like her it would just wobble and veer off to the left or right, she couldn't work out, so she decided the best plan was to just hit it and hope for the best.

She struck her ball hard and, like it had been shot out of a cannon, the ball bounced and raced across the grass, snaking slightly as it trundled across the green and veered off to miss the hole by a couple of feet, hitting Samantha's shoe and rolling a couple of feet away.

Samantha smiled sympathetically and, placing her bag and the flag down, she came over to Nicola as she reached her ball.

'No, no, no, your stance is all wrong,' she told her as she came up behind Nicola and put her arms around her, holding her club with her as she gently wrapped her hands around Nicola's. 'Let me show you.' Nicola blushed a little as Samantha continued. 'You grip it like this and...' They went through a swing together. 'See! You have to follow through.'

Samantha stepped away as Nicola suddenly became all overcome with an excited, self-conscious passion, which made her feel all giddy inside and for a moment she feared she was about to swoon as she gasped for breath and went all weak at the knees, before she was able to get control of her senses and recovered her posture.

'You couldn't show me that again?' Nicola asked as Samantha then came behind her again and laid her hands over Nicola's. Together, they rehearsed the motions of putting, before Samantha returned to the hole, picked up the flag and waited.

Nicola composed herself with two deep breaths. She

looked at the ball, then to the hole and imagined her stroke, the putter pushing through the ball. After checking her feet were well apart and her head was down, she gently swung her body and club as one, repeating in her body what her mind had seen, the putter drifted on, into and through the ball, which rolled on, steady and in contact with the green all the time, drifting down to the hole's edge and tipping over and in.

'Atta girl!' Samantha beamed broadly with pride.

Nicola smiled, as she came over to the hole and picked up her ball from the cup.

Then, flag replaced, clubs in their bags, they together headed off to the next hole.

*

O'Brian stood in front of the Riley looking furtively around, ensuring that no one was watching them. O'Keefe, his two feet sticking out from under the side of the Riley's engine area, wriggled slightly as the sound of metal being sawn rang out.

*

They had reached the eighth hole, the last of their short game. Samantha took some sand from the box by the marker and made a small mound, her tee, on which she set her ball as Nicola watched, leaning on her golf bag.

Samantha eyed her ball and drew her heavy wooden club to the ball twice before she looked along the fairway. She steadied her stance, checked and controlled her breathing, noted in her mind the way the wind was blowing and how strong it was from the trees and the flag. Then she pulled the club back slowly and struck the ball with one huge swing that rippled through her.

It soared high into the sky. For a moment she thought she might lose it against the small patch of white, lamb's-tail clouds that hung in the distance, but then against the background of the trees she saw it come bouncing down onto the grass, on the centre of the fairway, nearly two thirds the distance to the green.

Nicola picked up her sand and made ready her tee.

'Do you fancy a quick one before heading off?' Samantha asked as Nicola quickly looked around.

'There's a lot of people about? But I'm sure we'd be safe in the rough!'

'I was thinking on the patio,' Samantha replied.

'Isn't that a bit public?' Nicola was a bit surprised.

'Bar's members only,' Samantha reminded her and for a moment, Nicola blushed. 'Though they do have a steward so we could have a swift G and T before dinner.'

Nicola sighed then smiled. 'Ab-so-lute-ly.' Then she readied her club behind her ball and tried to get her mind back on the game as, even with all Samantha's helpful hints, golf just didn't come naturally to her.

*

O'Brian was still keeping a furtive watch as the sawing under the car suddenly stopped. Hearing the scraping of boots on the gravel he turned back as a worn-out O'Keefe slipped out from under the car.

'You done?' O'Brian asked.

'Very nearly.'

'Come on. Before somebody sees us!'

O'Keefe scrambled to his feet and they both quickly ran back to the bushes just as Albert emerged from the side entrance of the clubhouse, crossing over to the car with a slight stagger.

He could see his reflection in the passenger side window and adjusted his jacket to make himself appear smarter, just as Sam and Nicola appeared from the main entrance. Carrying their golf bags and golf shoes, giggling and with a wiggle in their step, they briskly sauntered over to the car.

He waited for them to reach him and as they did so they put their bags down in front of him.

'Enjoy yourselves, Miss?'

'And how,' Samantha replied. 'Wouldn't you agree I've improved your stroke?!'

'I was always having trouble in the rough,' Nicola began, 'but now thanks to Sam's tips, I can flick my way out of any amount of wiry undergrowth or hook my way out of any sand trap.'

'Bunker, Miss.' He almost burped.

'Ab-so-lute-ly!' Nicola replied as Albert then took the bags to the back of the car and stowed them away while Samantha and Nicola waited by the door.

'Albert. We'll give the Cœur d'Or's engines a test tomorrow then make our plans to take her down to Cannes,' Samantha informed him. 'We'll have to go back to London first and pack ourselves some more clothes.'

'I could wire ahead and have someone from your father's staff pack them for us, Miss?' he asked, closing the box lid down and fastening its two leather straps.

'No,' she replied. 'We'll do it ourselves. We must pack right. It's positively warm down there in the south.'

'Don't I know it!' Nicola exclaimed with a wicked grin.

'Very good, Miss.' He emerged around to the side of the car. 'Do you wish to go straight back to the cottage, Miss?'

'Please, Albert,' Samantha replied as he opened the door for her and Nicola before he made his way around to the driver's seat.

The roar of the Riley's engine echoed the first time of asking and the car slipped backwards across the gravel. Then there was the sound of the familiar clunk as she was put into first gear and slowly they drove off, heading back to their cottage.

16

The Riley sped along the narrow, country road between the high embankments. The thick green bushes swept by as snug in the back under their tartan travel rug sat Samantha and Nicola. The road was a little bumpy, but nothing that the large coach springs couldn't handle and so Albert found the empty road relaxing, which was just as well, as he wasn't feeling all that alert and really just wanted to go to sleep.

From the side door pocket, Samantha took out her hip flask and flipped the lid to take a sip, before offering it to Nicola who also took a sip.

The Riley leapt over the brow of a steep hill and started to gather pace.

Albert could feel that the steering was beginning to feel a little woolly in his hands, as if the front wheels were not in full contact with the road. He depressed the footbrake. It fell flat against the floor, but the engine continued to race and the car was still gathering speed.

Suddenly he wasn't feeling all that merry as an icy chill ran down his spine.

The Riley swayed slightly, almost hitting the bank as he started to lose control. He was fighting with the wheel. He couldn't let it go, as the whole car was beginning to sway erratically on its springs.

Samantha put her flask back in the side pocket. She could sense something was wrong. The car was weaving wildly, throwing them from side to side, and glancing at Nicola she could see the fear etched across her face.

'You know I'm no bluenose, Albert,' Samantha called, betraying her own fear in her voice. 'In fact, I'm quite a fan of speed in my Alvis and I have even raced Napiers but I'm quite sure this vehicle is not built for it.'

'I quite agree, Miss,' Albert's trembling voice echoed in reply.

'Ab-so-lute-ly, and I must say, if we go any faster, Nicky and I are in great danger of bruising our BTM's!'

'And that won't do, will it, Miss?'

'Then may I suggest you slow down?'

'May I advise you, Miss…' he pulled at the wheel, it almost slipping from his grasp, '…with all due respect, that's what I'm trying to do!' He pulled on the handbrake, but nothing happened.

'You don't mean…?'

'I'm afraid so, Miss. Our brakes are out!!'

The Riley weaved across the road left to right then back again, knocking up puffs of dirt as the car violently, scraped the banks, as it continued to accelerate down the hill.

She had to think fast, to take charge. She pulled herself up using the seat in front of her and leant over to Albert. 'Change down!' she instructed him. 'Put her in second. Let the engine slow us.'

'Yes, Miss.' He started to crunch down through the

gears.

The engine screamed in protest, the car's body shuddered and the engine whined louder and louder as the Riley began to slow, weaving slightly. Albert fought hard with the wheel as Samantha and Nicola, holding each other's hands for comfort and support, watched nervously, helplessly praying inside that he could hold on.

As the hill bottomed out, the Riley slowed more rapidly and Albert put the car into neutral. They coasted along until they came to a gentle stop and the engine died. Albert shakily clambered out of the car and, with his hands still shaking, he opened the door for Samantha and Nicola to get out.

'My overalls, please, Albert,' she instructed him, taking off her gloves.

He crossed his way around to the back of the car as Nicola turned nervously to Sam.

'Do you think something's gone wrong with the car?' she asked.

'Hardly!'

Albert shook the overalls out from the boot and rolled them up, towards the ankles, as he helped Samantha step into them. She fastened the buttons up the front quickly before taking off her golfing hat and handing it to Nicola. She carefully slipped herself under the car sliding along until she was under the engine.

'Horsefeathers!' she screamed, and Nicola blushed with embarrassment as she caught Albert's eye. Samantha scrambled back out and stood up, adding, 'As I thought.' The anger flashed across her eyes as Nicola asked, 'What's happened?'

'Someone's cut the brake cable.'

'Who would have done such a thing?' Nicola asked, still trembling slightly. 'Don't they know it's dangerous?'

'I except so.' Samantha seethed, then a thought struck her. 'But the question we really have to ask ourselves is why?'

17

The taxi dropped them off at their cottage and after Albert had collected some wood and lit a small fire to take away the evening chill, Samantha and Nicola dressed in something more casual for lounging around the cottage and relaxed as they waited for Albert to prepare their supper.

Samantha was sitting in one armchair looking at the fire, watching the thin wisps of smoke, pirouette and dance across the wood, interrupted by the flickering flames before flittering up into the darkness of the chimney.

A cigarette was in her long, red holder, which was resting between her fingers like a pencil, and she drew on it occasionally, but for the most part she was letting it burn itself down. In her other hand, she was nursing a glass of whisky as she pondered all that had happened to her that day.

Nicola was sitting in the other chair with a steaming hot mug of cocoa in her hands, her feet up under her as she melted down into her seat and warmed herself by the fire, equally perplexed by all that had happened.

The fire crackled as the sap in the wood boiled and spat. Samantha concentrated on the dancing orange and yellow flames, hoping to see something, an inspiration, anything that would give her a clue as to why all this was happening to her. But no matter how hard she thought about everything, there was nothing she could think of.

Albert entered from the kitchen.

'I've just called the garage, Miss,' he informed her as she shook herself from her thoughts and turned to him. 'They say it will be ready tomorrow evening, Miss.'

'You mean we could be stuck here for another day!' Samantha sighed heavily. 'I was hoping to be back in London by Tuesday!'

'We could move down to a five-star hotel on the front, Miss?'

'But I want to be back amongst our gay society, Albert.' She stretched a little as she moved back into her seat. 'I want to have a gay old time amongst the clubs of London's West End, not freezing in the south easterlies of the south west!'

'It's the best they can do. They are a small garage,' he apologized, but she knew really he had done all he could.

'We could take a train?' Nicola offered, wanting to be back in the safe surrounds of their home. She waited as Samantha thought for a moment.

'We haven't really packed anything suitable to wear on the train,' she muttered more for herself than for the benefit of the others. 'I wasn't anticipating not having my car!'

'I'm sure the garage is doing their best, Miss,' he assured her.

'Or we could sail back to London?' Nicola suggested, taking a sip of her cocoa.

'Miss?'

'The Cœur d'Or,' Nicola reminded him.

'Are you sure, Miss? Neither of us have ever piloted a boat before,' he replied, nodding discreetly to Samantha as she took a sip of her drink, the ice rattling in her glass.

'But I know how to sail her!' Nicola exclaimed, realising that she quite liked the idea and eagerly wanted them to give it a try.

'Quite, Miss, but I'm sure she's too big!' He voiced his doubts, wishing not to dampen her enthusiasm yet at the same time mindful of the fact that the sea could be a cruel and unforgiving place for a group of novices, with its rip tides, its hidden rocks and unpredictable weather. Drowning at sea, he reminded himself, wasn't in his job description.

'Nonsense!' she scoffed. 'She's automatic and it only takes one to steer her. Growing up near the docks, with sailors and fishermen as my father's main source of income, I learnt a lot about steering a tiller-driven boat. The foreign sailors liked to show me their bridges every time Father and I were on board. I've even been allowed to steer the odd boat and barge along the Tyne and, although I've never been to sea, some of the Russian sailors used to like to show me their charts over a bottle or two of vodka. I understand and can read a sea chart easily.'

'Now you're on the trolley, baby.' Samantha smiled, raising her glass as in a toast.

'You can bring me my food at the wheel and if we moor up at night and in any bad weather, I think I can make it without having to buy too many seasickness pills before we cast off.'

'And what about the engines?' he asked. 'What if they should have problems en route?'

'The lights and things are run off a petrol engine,' Samantha replied, as she began to warm to the idea, 'which isn't too dissimilar to a car's. It would be just like looking after my Alvis.'

'What about the drive engines, Miss?' He still wasn't convinced. 'I suppose they're diesel?'

'So what if they are?' she replied. 'That's all about pressure and compression. I know how they work! I could maintain either on our voyage and the kitchen…'

'Galley,' Nicola corrected her.

'My apologies, baby, the galley is well stocked and easy to work in and I'm sure, as long as the champagne is well chilled and there's enough lemons for our afternoon tea, we'll have a swell old time. Don't be such a wet blanket, Albert. Can you really see any serious problems occurring?' She took a quick sip of her drink as Albert desperately tried to think of one. 'That is to say,' she added, 'It's not like we're really leaving dear old Blighty, is it? It's not like we're going to be sailing round some foreign waters! These are British waters. If we get lost, we can just pull into the nearest port and ask the way! So what could possibly go wrong?'

Put like that, it seemed so simple, and he shrugged. 'I still think it would be better to hire a little car now to get us back to London and then hire a proper crew to sail her down to Cannes later, Miss.'

'Where's your spirit of adventure, Albert?' Samantha asked.

'I fear my wage is a few shillings short for that, Miss.'

Suddenly there was a loud smashing sound of breaking plate glass, as a stone came crashing through the lounge window, sending shards of splintering fragments cascading all over the little table and carpet. Nicola dropped her mug, spilling the milky cocoa all over the side of the chair and onto the rug as she started. Samantha hurriedly leapt from her chair and raced over to look out of the window, reaching it as Albert rushed out the door.

'What happened?' Nicola asked, a little shaken as Samantha crossed over to the stone and picked it up. She looked at it curiously.

'It's a stone, with some paper wrapped   around

it.' She shrugged, feeling more confused than angry.

'Who'd want to wrap a stone? Not like the glass was going to damage it,' Nicola remarked as Albert returned, closing and locking the door behind him and drawing across the deadbolts.

'I can't see anyone out there, Miss. They must have gone down the cliff lane.'

Sam unravelled the paper.

'There's some writing on the paper.' Nicola pointed to the sheet. Samantha looked at it as she handed the stone to Albert.

'R.J. Jackson and Son, Glaziers, 129, High Street, Torquay,' she read. 'Well, if that's how he goes about advertising his business, I'm surprised he gets any!!'

Albert placed the stone down on the dining table.

'There's something on the other side,' Nicola added as Samantha turned it round and read.

'Leave now, forget the Cœur d'Or if you know what's good for you.' She turned to Nicola. 'So it wasn't from Jackson and Son's after all! It's a warning to keep away from the boat. But why?' She was even more confused. What was it that was so special about that boat. It was a nice boat she had to admit, but what was it she hadn't seen?

'Shall I call for the police, Miss?' Albert asked, bringing her back from her thoughts.

'And tell them what?' she asked. 'Someone's thrown a stone through our window?'

'But, this and the car, Miss. Your life is definitely in danger, Miss,' he reminded her nervously.

'Probably.' She shrugged, quite enjoying the adrenaline rush coursing through her veins, 'but at the very best if they catch the culprit, he'll be fined a shilling for his troubles.' She began to weigh up all that had happened and now this. At last something was beginning to take shape. She didn't know what but her curiosity was aroused. 'No,' she defiantly replied. Turning to them both, a devilish smile crept across her lips. 'There's a mystery here and it centres around the Cœur d'Or. I think before we turn this over to the police, we should investigate it a little further.' She took a sip of her drink and a fiery sparkle twinkled in her eyes. 'So, someone's tried to kill all of us and this warning to stay away from the Cœur. Well, no one tells me what I can and can't do and I take exception to people trying to kill me.' She turned to Albert. 'Looks like we are going to be staying a little longer in Torquay, don't you think, Albert?'

'I think so, Miss.'

'Then tomorrow, after we've picked up our car, let's see what these bimbos are doing with Sylvie's Cœur.'

18

O'Hare emerged from one of the large warehouses along the quay. The setting sun was low on the horizon. It was late, and he was tired and hungry. He quickly glanced furtively around, ensuring no one was watching but he couldn't see anyone. The quay was empty but for a couple of gulls sitting on some lobster pots and a couple more squawking overhead.

Then he pulled his jacket tighter around him, dug his hands into his pockets and quickly made his way over to the main dock area where O'Brian sat waiting in the driver's seat of a long, soft-topped, red Sunbeam. The hood was up but the side panels were down.

O'Hare checked that there was no one around to overhear him.

'Did you put the frighteners on those flappers?' he asked.

'I sure did.' O'Brian grinned, then shaking his head, added, 'but they're still there tonight.'

'What is it with these women?' O'Hare asked himself. 'You would have thought after they survived a near fatal car accident that they would have got the message by now!'

From his inside pocket, he took out a packet of cigarettes and helped himself to one. Then after putting the packet away, he took out his matchbox, struck a match and lit his cigarette. He took two puffs before snuffing out the flame with a flick of his wrist and tossing the match away. He was beginning to feel the pressure. He liked it when things were simple, when things ran to plan, but these two women were like the grit in the cogs of a well-oiled machine, making it stutter, making it struggle and making him feel very uneasy indeed. He had enough stress in his life. He didn't need any more and he didn't need anything that might expose his network to the police. He had to act and he knew he had to act fast.

'Look.' He turned back to O'Brian. 'You're going to have to bump them off .'

'Won't we be bringing too much attention on us if we do?'

'As long as the Police are looking the other way tonight I don't care, we can move operations down the coast if we need to. I'll get O'Keefe to handle that before we return.'

'If you're sure?'

O'Hare nodded taking a drag of his cigarette. 'We've got to move everything with tomorrow night's tide and we can't have them snooping about till then. If they come round in the morning after we're gone, that pair are bound to tell the police.' He took another drag of his cigarette. 'Take O'Keefe with you. He's got the tommy gun. If they don't leave in the morning, do what you have to do.'

'What will you be doing?' O'Brian asked.

'Taking out a bit of insurance just in case.'

O'Brian nodded and then started the car as O'Hare

stepped back to watch. O'Brian clunked the Sunbeam into first gear and slowly drove away.

*

They had slept in that morning and had a late breakfast. Albert left Samantha and Nicola to read the newspapers with some tea in the living room, while he was washing up some plates in the kitchen.

It was much smaller than he was used to. Basically there was just a small cupboard in which to keep all the crockery, a table to prep the food and a large sink with a draining board next to it. There was a second small sink to prep the vegetables in. He stood by the larger sink, the water full of thick white suds, his shirt sleeves rolled up, as with a sponge on a stick, he took the large white plates one by one from under all the white suds and wiped both sides of the plates with the sponge before stacking them on the draining board, concave sides down. The soapy water drained into the grooves and dribbled back into the larger sink.

He had just begun to clean a matching tea cup when he heard a car horn at the front of the cottage. He put the cup back in the water and hung the sponge over the single tap with the string at the end of the handle. Picking up a tea towel from the back of a chair that was pushed under the table, he carefully dried his hands, rolled down his sleeves, put on his butler's jacket and left the kitchen.

He made his way out to the lounge and was surprised to see that neither of the two young ladies were there. The newspapers had been left draped over the arms of the two armchairs and the tea cups were both on the floor beside them, but Samantha and Nicola were gone. At first he thought they were already outside with the taxi but then he noticed that the front door was still bolted, so after slipping the bolt back he opened the door.

At the front, sitting on the driveway of the cottage,

was a blue Wolseley taxi, the driver waiting patiently behind the wheel. He turned to the door as Albert opened it. Albert signalled to him that he knew he was there and the driver waved back, relieved he had arrived at the right place, as Albert went back inside.

He pushed the door to, turning to the sound of heavy rushing footsteps as Nicola and Samantha quickly came running down the stairs, straightening their slightly rumpled clothes as they came down.

'Taxi's here, Miss,' he informed them both, as Samantha straightened her cloche hat, tucking some of her hair under the brim.

'Good, Albert,' she replied a little flustered as Nicola suddenly paused to quickly re-attach one of her suspender belts that had come detached from her stocking.

'Where shall I meet you in town, Miss, after I've picked up the Riley?' he asked.

'We were thinking of having a spot to eat at Dolby's Seaside Café,' Samantha replied. 'Nicky was saying they do fish and chips there and there is a place to sit and eat them on the premises.'

'Very good, Miss.' He bowed slightly. 'I shall meet you there.'

He stood back holding open the door for them as the two women rushed past him and over to the taxi.

He crossed with them to the taxi and as the taxi driver reached out to the handle and opened the door, pushing it slightly to him, Albert held it open for Samantha and Nicola to climb in. Once they were settled, he slammed the door, and headed back to the cottage to watch from the doorway. The taxi's engine roared back into life and, as it pulled away, Albert went back inside closing the door behind him.

As the taxi began to make its way along the narrow country lane, the red Sunbeam soft-top began to follow, just a little way behind.

19

Torquay seafront was set back in a bay, at one end the harbour, with an esplanade that stretched west from the harbour, until the town met the cliffs as they reached back out towards the sea. Between the sea and the road along which the trams trundled, there was a small bowling green with its pavilion by the harbour's dividing wall, opening out to a large promenade with a grey, stone seawall protecting it from the beach below.

Occasionally there were gaps in the wall, with platforms pushed out towards the beach. Two sets of steps, either end of the platform, stretched down to the soft sands below. Across the road, facing the esplanade there was a long row of four to five floor hotels and boarding houses, from the high class to the middle class, all gleaming with their immaculately painted window frames and doors, evoking the cleanliness and richness of this quintessential English seaside resort.

Along the front, those enjoying the warm, liquid sunshine meandered around, passing the street vendors with their tricycles and push-along barrows, selling food, or from their trays, suspended by a strap around their necks, vending anything from matches to balloons.

The taxi crossed over the tram tracks to park against the kerb of the esplanade, halfway along the walk. The taxi driver watched as from the back Samantha opened the door and stepped out, to be greeted by the soft breeze sweeping in off the sea, followed by Nicola. Samantha leant through his passenger door to pay him. Nicola closed the rear door and took a few steps towards the sea wall.

The taxi pulled away as the Sunbeam came to a stop a few yards behind where they stood.

Samantha came over to Nicola, placed her arm in hers and together they walked over to the sea wall, where they stood to breathe in the invigorating salty air. A tiny bell rang out as an ice-cream seller in his blue-and-white striped shirt and straw boater on his tricycle came to a gentle stop, the box on front ornately decorated in blue and white with 'Mario's Ices' written big and bold across the centre of each box panel. A young family came over to him to buy ice creams. By the wall a little way from him a man with a huge bunch of balloons looped around his left arm on strings and a tray with flags for sandcastles hanging from his neck stood watching the other families passing by, offering them his balloons for a farthing.

*

O'Brian pulled on the handbrake and adjusted the regulator as O'Keefe behind him leant over the bench seat. Beside him, there was a lump under a travel rug and he took the rug off to reveal the tommy gun.

He pulled the gun up onto his lap and slid the bolt across the top, back towards the trigger, in a single motion. The gun clicked, now cocked and ready. Its large round drum between the trigger and the forward handgrip made the gun feel heavy, but O'Keefe was as strong as an ox and it was like it was made of balsawood in his hands.

He turned to look where Samantha and Nicola were, his attention was drawn to them alone as he calmly instructed O'Brian in a cold, slow voice.

'Keep it nice and slow.'

'But all these people?'

'That can't be helped.' O'Keefe grinned mockingly as he turned to look at O'Brian via the rear-view mirror. 'For the cause.'

O'Brian nodded his agreement. For any cause there must be sacrifice and then, as the dull clunk rang out, he put the car into first gear, set the regulator again and released the handbrake and clutch slowly.

*

With a slight jolt the saloon car began to creep forward.

Samantha slipped out of Nicola's arm and as she turned, she could see the ice cream vendor. It was a warm day and she could see he had some wafers in their stand on the side of his box. She felt they deserved a nice refreshing ice cream. She watched as the family were each in turn handed one of those lovely looking, loaded wafers, the children's drenched with butterscotch sauce swirled over the top of them.

'You know what would be the bee's knees right now?' She turned to Nicola, who gave a quizzical look. 'An ice cream.'

Nicola smiled as they both walked over to the ice cream seller. Behind them, the saloon car continued to slowly creep forward.

The family turned to walk away as Samantha and Nicola stepped up to take their turn.

'Ladies. And what may I get you?' the ice cream vendor asked in a broad Devonshire accent.

'Do you have any peppermint favour?' Samantha asked.

'Certainly, madam.' he replied enthusiastically as Samantha turned to Nicola.

'Think I'd like to try that too,' she added, making Samantha smile.

*

His hands felt slippery on the steering wheel as he watched the girls and glanced at the road ahead. He could feel the beads of sweat forming under his fringe but he couldn't wipe them away. He had to stay focused and keep the car steady. He heard behind him the clatter of the tommy gun being lifted as O'Keefe brought the stock up to his shoulder, leaning the front of the gun on the edge of the car.

Then, once he was settled, the muzzle just protruding over the edge of the car door, he leant forward over the side, the tommy gun almost pulling him over as he raised it, looking down the line of the gun holding it close to his cheek, rear sight to foresight. He waited as the car continued to creep forward, waiting until the moment Samantha would appear in his sights.

*

He decided to change his grip on the balloons. The breeze was beginning to come off the land and was making them bump against him. Carefully, he began to pull them down towards him.

*

O'Keefe flexed his grip. The girls were in his sights. He squeezed the handgrip and the trigger together in his hand.

*

Suddenly a balloon popped and a little startled, Samantha looked round, her warm smile turning to terror as she saw the tommy gun levelled at her. Without a moment's hesitation, she dived forward, pushing Nicola to the floor, to land on top of her as the bright flashes began to erupt from its muzzle.

*

Instantly, as the gun's muzzle began to flash, O'Keefe's view of the girls was obscured. He pulled on the trigger and, capable of six hundred rounds per minute, the thirty-round drum, emptied its bullets within a blink of an eye. The kick of each round being expelled made the gun judder in his hands and he couldn't hold it tight to him anymore, the gun for the few seconds it fired seeming to dance in his hands, spraying the bullets everywhere.

*

The clattering chatter of the gun and the rain of shell cases falling to the pavement, filled her ears with their deafening echo as Samantha laid protectively over Nicola. The bullets sprayed the ice cream seller's tricycle. The ice cream seller was hit and recoiled in a circle as he fell dead to the ground. The balloon seller, diving for cover, let go of all his balloons and as they floated away, they separated from their bunch, the wind taking them high and out towards the sea.

The saloon's engine roared and O'Brian clunked it into second gear as it began to speed away. O'Keefe, new drum in his gun, looking backwards, kept firing at them as they passed Mario's tricycle until the magazine was empty.

Chips of stone erupted around them, as bullet after bullet struck the slabs. Then O'Keefe slid back inside the saloon, the last of his rounds having rippled like hail across the pavement, almost hitting the family. The children screamed in terror, the car roared around past a tram and slipped away up a nearby side street.

All was quiet but for a constant ringing in her ears.

Samantha peered up from under the tricycle and through the spokes of the wheel she could see the car disappearing down the road.

She felt a little unsteady as she stood up, as if she was full of sand and it was all running down to her ankles. She helped Nicola up then started to dust herself down.

'You think that was meant for us?' Nicola asked, dusting herself down too.

'Ab-so-lute-ly,' Samantha replied.

She noticed how Nicola's hands trembled and how pale her face now looked, and then she looked at her own hands, constantly fidgeting as if they had a life of their own.

She felt cold.

She felt numb.

Her heart was racing and yet, everything seemed to be in echo, the sounds, and the light, everything seemed detached, unreal.

She knew she should feel sad for the dead man, yet, she couldn't feel anything not even for him, it was as if the shock had overwhelmed her and placed her life and senses in neutral, the emotions, the fear, the grief would come later.

It was then she noticed there was a tear in the hem of her new summer dress, and it struck her at once, just how close some of the bullets must have been and how close she had come to being another victim.

Her hands still shook, and looking to Nicola she

could see her ashen face staring back, eyes wide and that there were tear stains upon her cheeks, she comforted her, holding her gently by the arm and with a thin reassuring smile whispered, 'I'm just glad you're fine.'

'I'm glad you are as well.' Nicola replied smiling back, her voice trembling, unable to hide her anxiety.

Samantha looked to the direction of the Harbour, 'Now I really want to discover what it is that's so important about this boat!'

20

The Wolseley taxi pulled up outside the cottage and as the driver tooted his horn, the door opened and Albert appeared, in a regular jacket and wearing his bowler hat. The driver leant through his window to open the rear passenger door as Albert locked up. He crossed to the taxi and as he climbed in, he cried, 'Merryweather Garage, please.'

'Right you are, squire.'

Albert shut the door as the driver put the taxi into first and slowly turned the car round in the yard before, with a roar of the engine, they headed off back down the lane, the taxi beeping twice as they approached the narrow corner a few yards down.

A few moments passed. Then from the bushes of the field opposite, O'Hare emerged through the thick hawthorn hedge with a small rucksack on his back and pushing his bike. He placed the bike on the road, quickly hopped on and rode up to the cottage's front garden.

He leant the bike on the wall near the front door and then knocked on the door twice. He waited and much to his relief no one answered. He glanced around him. There was no one about and leaving the bike where it was, he gingerly made his way around the side of the cottage to the back.

There was a small Dutch-style door at the back, next to the log pile, and after checking around him again that there was no one about, he took from inside his jacket a long, slim, metal rule, which he slipped under the latch and jolted it up sharply. He smiled as he heard the latch slip. He slipped the rule back inside his jacket and glancing behind him, he quickly pushed the door open as he stepped forward and nearly fell headlong over the bottom half of the door which was still held in place by a bolt.

He pushed himself back up and cursed himself under his breath as he slid back the bolt and then entered the kitchen.

He slipped his rucksack off as he continued through into the living room and set the bag down on the dining table, the leaves of which had now been folded down, and casually, with no sense of urgency, he set about unfastening the two straps. Then from inside the rucksack he took out a long crowbar and a flat chisel.

Leaving the bag where it was and holding the tools in each hand, he began to walk along the room, pressing down on the floor with each step until, just as he reached the foot of the stairs, he heard the groaning sound of an old, tired floorboard protesting at being stepped on.

Quickly he found the end, and using the crowbar at the short face where it butted onto the next board, he forced it up an inch or so. He then slipped in the chisel to give him the extra purchase he needed under the crowbar and lifted that part of the floorboard clear. The nails pulled and the wood squealed as they were torn from the joist, but with his thick muscled arms he found it easy to do. Next he followed the floorboard to the next joist and continued to lift it out bit by bit until the whole board was freed.

Leaving the tools where they were, he crossed back to his bag and took from it a large windup clock, with a double bell on top, to which a couple of wires were attached and connected to a battery, all tightly wound round six long sticks of dynamite.

He checked the time on his watch. It had just gone noon and he set the clock's alarm to twelve, before setting the clock to the right time. With its fixed key in its back, he wound the clock spring fully and then set on the alarm button. Before lowering the device into the hole between the joists, he crossed back to his bag to take out a pack of cotton wadding normally used between the planks on the yachts to cushion the noise and packed that all around the bomb.

This done, he replaced the floorboard, took his tools back to the bag and took out a well-used, heavy, two-pound hammer and gently knocked the nails back in.

As he stood on the finished board, the squeak was gone, and he was mildly impressed with his work, though he doubted any of them would notice that there was no longer a squeaky board at the foot of the stairs, he assured himself. Even if they did, they wouldn't know why and at any rate, by the time he and his boys were safely out of harbour and on their way to Ireland, those nosey flappers were going to be doing the Charleston to the sounds of harps.

He checked he had everything packed away in his bag and that nothing was left behind that shouldn't have been. Then, as he slipped the rucksack back on, he left via the kitchen, remembering to put the bolt on the lower half of the Dutch door, and headed back round to pick up his bike and cycle all the way back to the boatyard.

THE CŒUR D'OR MYSTERY

*

Just off from the long main room, with its counter and fish fat fryer fizzling away, in a small ante-room, decorated in the same tiles from floor to ceiling with white tiles above a brown ceramic dado rail and brown tiles below it to the floor, Samantha, Nicola and Albert were sitting on the long wooden benches around a very rustic wooden table with salt and vinegar shakers in the middle. They each had in front of them their opened-out newspaper bundles of chips and some fish, which they ate with small wooden forks.

Over the white tiles in the middle of the wall, just like a painting, there was in bright, gaudy red with gold around the edges and red lettering 'Dolby's Fish Bar' in fancy gothic script, inside a matching red-and-gold frame. There were a couple of tables as well as some bench seating around the smaller room, but only Samantha, Nicola and Albert were there, illuminated under the dim, yellowish glow of the three electric lamps on the one fitting that sat centrally in the ceiling and seemed largely to be only illuminating brightly the plain plaster above.

The frying room was a hive of activity as the customers, largely working class in their rough more practical best, huddled along the tiled wall in a 'U'-shaped queue from the door round to counter, taking their penny's worth of fish and halfpenny of chips, before scurrying off into the chill of the late evening sea breeze, that was whistling in through the almost constantly open door, never really staying shut for long before the next customer came in.

Somewhere in the queue, the piercing sound of a baby crying and the coarse banter droning on in the background made Samantha shudder as if some icy water had just dribbled down her spine.

'So, what did the police say happened, Miss?' Albert asked loading a chip on his fork.

'Typical blinkered thinking,' Samantha replied as she speared some fish onto her fork. 'I explained to them what I thought happened, over and over again, and all they would say was, it was probably a dispute over vending pitches . Apparently, some other company used to sell ices there. They said it's been worse since after the war because there were so many guns brought back as souvenirs.' She ate her fish, taking out her annoyance by spearing a long soggy chip.

'Rather an extreme way to make a protest, Miss?'

'And how!' she agreed as Nicola shook some more salt onto her chips. 'If everyone behaved like that, the streets of Britain would be swamped with shootings left right and centre! No, the police are way off on this one. Though trying to explain it might be to do with something else without knowing what that something else might be, made it hard for them to believe me. I'm afraid to have to say it, but they've settled for the undemanding alternative, yet I'm sure Sylvie's boat has got something to do with it.' Samantha shuddered again as the child's crying grew louder. 'Can't she do something about that child crying?'

'It's teething,' Nicola replied as she munched on her large mouthful of chips. She'd abandoned the politeness of using a fork and was now using her fingers to eat them three at a time. Samantha sighed, showing her frustration. Nicola added as she finished a mouthful, 'She needs to put some whiskey, rum or something like that, on its gums, to take the pain way.'

Samantha took out her hipflask from her handbag and passed it over to Albert.

'Give her some of this, Albert.'

'Very good, Miss,' he replied unfastening screw lid and flipping it open as he stood and headed out into the frying room.

Samantha ate another chip.

'I'm so glad I don't have one of those,' she remarked.

'So am I!' Nicola agreed almost as if her soul had

been gripped by some unspeakable terror.

'I'm too young.' Samantha defended herself. 'Anyway, life should be for living. It's about having fun and being gay. Why would anyone want to tie themselves down with one of those things?'

'Though I do appreciate that they are useful.'

'In what way?' Samantha asked.

'They keep the human race going,' Nicola reminded her as she scooped up and ate a bit of fish.

'Suppose. But really. Don't think me a wet blanket for being so harsh but that noise and those smells, do children really have to be so…' She struggled for the right word. '…messy?'

Nicola grinned sympathetically and ate another chip just as the baby stopped crying and the mellow hum of facile conversation drifted over in its place.

'Looks like your remedy works!'

Samantha was impressed as Nicola, with a little pride swelling her chest replied, 'It's what Father always advises.'

Albert returned and sat down, screwing the lid back on the hipflask, which he passed back to Samantha and, as she put it back in her handbag, she resumed her train of thought.

'As I was saying, I'm sure Sylvie's boat has got something to do with all this and I think whatever it is that whoever they are, are using her boat for, must be needing to do whatever it is soon. Or else why would they be trying ever more desperately to stop us getting near that boat? After all, nothing as far as I can tell happened until Sylvie decided to sell it and they didn't start to take any real drastic action until after we agreed to take it down to Cannes for her.'

'I agree, Miss,' Albert began. He tried to spear a rather soggy chip that just wouldn't attach to his fork and, after agreeing with himself that the battle was lost, picked it up with his fingers instead before continuing, 'but if we just try and board the boat now, won't they be ready for us?'

'Whoever they are, they're a serious bunch,' Nicola reminded them. 'We'd never be able to take them on straight!'

'And how,' Samantha agreed. 'I know we don't know much about these birds, other than they're desperate. But I'm not letting a bunch of bimbos cheat our friend Sylvie out of a couple of hundred thousand pounds. The Cœur d'Or's well worth that and she'll be able to move down to the south of France and start a new life somewhere like Nice or Saint-Tropez?'

'She certainly could do with all that dough,' Nicola commented. 'Wait!' An idea struck her. 'Now tell me if it's none of my beeswax but I've got an idea!'

21

The Harbour Master stood by his office window, his little stove burner, with its little blue flame, licking the bottom of his brown metal kettle. Next to it, into his brown tea pot he spooned from his battered old, brass-coloured, tin caddy a couple of spoonfuls of loose black tea. He replaced that behind his cup. From a bucket under the table filled with water and with a damp cloth over the top, he took out his bottle of milk and poured a little into his chipped, blue, enamel mug. As he put the bottle back in the bucket, his kettle began to boil.

With a tea towel in his hand, he lifted it off the burner and filled the teapot with water. Then he sat the kettle on the burner before extinguishing its flame and placing the lid on the teapot. Just at that moment he could hear the sound of raised voices and shouting, their voices echoing along the corridor as he took a bottle of whisky from his desk drawer and added some to his chipped enamel mug, just a little splash, so as not to curdle the milk.

He left the bottle by the milk and poured himself his tea, using a strainer over the mug to catch the loose leaves. Then, after a taste to make sure it was as strong as he liked it and feeling a little more relaxed, he carried his mug of tea with him as he left his office to investigate the ruckus he could still hear outside.

The harbour was dark as it was a cloudy night. The only light was the occasional gas lamp on the corner at the end of the warehouses and all he could see was some object along the quay moving and looking at some other dark shape in the harbour itself. He felt a little puzzled as he couldn't remember anything being berthed there and as he came closer, he tried to make the shape out.

He followed the voices and they led him to the quayside, where he was surprised to see that the Cœur d'Or was being moored alongside as a figure threw a rope to a man running along the quay to the rear of the boat.

Then he could see them clearly now in the lamps' overspill between the warehouse and the quay. The Harbour Master sighed and quickly made his way over to them. O'Hare was standing watching his other comrades mooring the boat.

'What's the meaning of this?' the Harbour Master asked as he reached O'Hare's side.

'We're loading her for the trip this weekend. Remember?'

'But you can't do that!' the Harbour Master protested sternly. 'You can't take her out! Not whilst those two flappers are here!'

'Why not?' O'Hare asked him with a shrug. 'Gilbert was our man. He was moving the money through the casino to buy us our guns and this boat. It may be in his name, but you know as well as I do, that she was designed and built to help us in our struggles.'

'Yes, I know.' The Harbour Master took a sip of his

tea. 'I helped set the deal up in the first place. But, as you know, the rules changed when Gilbert died in that race. The boat's his wife's now. You can't just sail her off without her permission.'

'Says who?' O'Hare snapped back. 'You?' he growled. 'Do I have to remind you you're one of us too?'

'Look.' He sipped some more tea. 'I can turn a blind eye to smuggling weapons to help free Ireland. I'm happy for the odd bomb blowing up innocent civilians and killing and maiming women and children. That's not my problem.' He shrugged. 'But using someone else's boat without their permission, now that's another matter! Regardless how noble the cause.'

'When the Free State marched our prisoners over the landmines to execute them, did that break us?' O'Hare flared at him bitterly, as his memory of those terrible times weighed heavily on his mind. 'No,' he growled. 'No one stands in our way, no matter what, until all Ireland is free, so I must have that boat!'

'I'm sorry. Call me an old stick in a mud, but there are lines you just don't cross.' The Harbour Master would not budge.

'And that will be your final word on the matter, will it?'

The Harbour Master took a sip of his tea as he thought for a moment.

'No.'

'So?' O'Hare asked.

'Unless you stop what you're doing,' the Harbour Master threatened, 'and put the boat back and let those two flappers conclude their business here so we can get on with things like we've been doing them before, then yes, I'll say no more. Otherwise, I'm getting the police.'

Suddenly, O'Hare drew a revolver out from under his jacket and before the Harbour Master could react, he pulled the trigger. The gun recoiled with a flash and a small cloud of smoke as he fired. Dropping his enamel mug, his tea spilled across the cobbles as it clattered around his feet and holding his stomach, the Harbour Master staggered back a couple of steps and sank slowly to the ground, dying.

O'Brian came running down the lowered gangplank over to O'Hare. He knelt beside the Harbour Master but he couldn't feel a pulse.

'You killed him!' O'Brian exclaimed with disbelief.

'I never liked the man.' O'Hare dismissed him as he carefully replaced his revolver.

'Well...' O'Brian rose to his feet. 'He liked you.'

O'Connor walked down the gangplank to join them.

'You did the right thing.' He slapped O'Hare approvingly on his back, adding, 'You're fine by me. The lush would have talked   sometime.'

'Come on.' O'Hare turned to them both. 'We can't stand here all night. High tide's at 23.40. We've got to be ready before then.'

O'Connor and O'Brian then picked up the Harbour Master's body and threw him off the quay before they all headed back up the gangplank and onto the boat.

22

The headlights searched along the wall, sweeping back to the Harbour Gate as the Riley came to a gentle stop, its brakes moaning. With the engine still running, the rear passenger door opened and out stepped Samantha, dressed in a dark trouser suit, soft canvas shoes and a black beret, followed by Nicola, who was similarly dressed, carrying a large, striped canvas bag.

Samantha came round to the front of the car and, leaning through the open driver's window as Nicola carefully closed the door silently behind her, she whispered, 'Albert? You know what to do?'

'Yes, Miss.' His voice echoed back from the blackness of the car and as they both stood back against the harbour wall, the familiar clunk of the car changing into first gear rang out as the revs picked up and the Riley started to pull away.

They watched him go around the corner, lit only by the mellow, flickering, green gas light fitted to the wall above them, its pipe slightly bent off true and with a twisted mantle, damaged in the last strong gale. Steeling herself, she turned to Nicola. 'Ready?'

Nicola nodded nervously and then together they tentatively made their way along the wall to the gates of the harbour, which they were surprised to find were still open and silently slipped inside.

*

The place had a creepy, almost ethereal, feel to it like a graveyard as they entered the largely dark and shadowy complex. It seemed very different, as if everything was alive and moving around them as they slowly picked their way along the wall and buildings, keeping close to them for fear of stepping too far into the dark and becoming lost or, worse, falling into the harbour.

Samantha could feel her heart knocking loudly against her ribs. She'd never felt so scared in all her life. Maybe it was a sign she was getting old, but she felt so vulnerable and was sure that somewhere in the darkness, eyes were watching her, but she had to carry on. They'd gone too far now and, anyway, their plan depended on her now and, as a shiver traced its way down her spine, she almost screamed as suddenly Nicola bumped into her. Swallowing her breath, she reassured herself that they were still both safe as no one knew they were there.

Soon they had reached the Harbour Master's building. The light from the window was still burning bright. Samantha took a deep breath and then, after quick reassuring glances at each other, together they summoned up all their courage and gingerly slipped in through the door and entered his office.

They were both surprised to find the room empty and as Nicola stood by the door, keeping a careful watch,

Samantha crossed to his desk, glancing quickly over the papers there, which meant nothing to her as she skimmed through them. Then, as she passed the teapot, she stopped to feel its sides.

'Pot's still warm. He must be about somewhere?' She noticed the bottle next to it.

'Ugh! Whisky in tea.' She grimaced at the very idea, how uncouth.

Nicola shielded her eyes from the harsh light as she peered out through the window.

'I think I see the Cœur d'Or by the quay.'

'Are you sure?' Samantha was surprised.

'No,' Nicola admitted, adding in her blunt northern tone, 'but it's the same shape and size, and there's a light up on its funnel and that's red and black like the Cœur's!'

'I thought he needed our permission to bring her into harbour and we've not given any instruction. We've not even decided when we're going to sail her to France yet.' She quickly went back to the table and started to flick though the sheets of paper until she found the dock's logbook. Quickly turning through the pages to the last entries, she read down and, turning back to Nicola, she continued, 'There's no large yachts due in. In fact, they only have one yacht, the Cœur d'Or, registered here.'

'Then it must be her,' Nicola declared. 'Then this must be it? Why they wanted us out the way!'

Samantha joined her at the office window and peered out.

'I wonder what they're up to.'

'Shouldn't we sneak down and take a closer look?' Nicola asked, tapping the strap to the canvas bag she still had draped over her shoulder.

'Ab-so-lute-ly, baby,' Samantha agreed and they then left the office together.

*

It took them what felt like an age to make their way through the darkness as they approached the dock. There were some packing cases near to where the Cœur d'Or was moored. As they got closer, they heard gruff voices and quickly Samantha and Nicola hid behind them.

Tentatively, they peered over the lowest case and watched as O'Hare and O'Brian were straining to carry a long crate off the back of a lorry parked next to the Sunbeam saloon car, which Samantha instantly recognised was the one used in the attempt to kill them along the seafront. They watched them intensely as the men took the box up the short gangplank and onto the Cœur d'Or.

'They're smugglers,' she whispered to Nicola. 'And they're using Sylvie's boat!'

'So that's the caper, the cads!' Nicola whispered back angrily as she punched the box in front of her.

'We need to get on board without them knowing.' Samantha looked around her, before she pointed to a hut behind them. 'Time to use our bag of tricks.'

Carefully they made their way over to the hut. It had a single large padlock holding a latch over an eye-loop. Samantha pointed to the bag and, as Nicola held it open for her, she took a crowbar from it. Holding the small curved end behind the latch, in one quick move she pushed the bar towards the door. There was an agonising cracking sound of the screws splitting and ripping themselves out of the wood, before the latch swung away and hung loose, still held to the door frame by the lock.

Nicola was surprised.

'How did you... ?'

'A schoolgirl in Paris during the war had only one of three ways of surviving, and I was too young for the first two.' Samantha grinned. 'So I learnt a few things that weren't on the curriculum. Saved me from starving.'

She put the crowbar back inside the bag.

'If we get through this, baby, and one night we're bored, sitting watching the wood burning in the fireplace,

I'll tell you all about it.'

Nicola smiled broadly as they gently pulled the door open and slipped silently inside.

The wheel of Samantha's lighter caught the spark off the flint and the bright, yellow-orange flame flickered, illuminating the shed. As Nicola pulled the door closed, Samantha looked around her. She was standing between a couple of packing cases full of ropes and on which there sat a couple of lobster pots. Before her, reaching back to the shed's far wall and jostling with each other as they spread out to the sides, were a number of other cases, as well as some old sails piled up on top of each other, several tarpaulins, pots of pitch that were well splashed and dried along the sides of the tins, old paint brushes that were brittle and useless and, on the shelf by the door, four brown bottles of white spirit.

Samantha held the light above her and she noticed near to her a kerosene hurricane lamp hanging on a short, thick, looped, black, rusting metal chain. As she lifted the glass, she could smell there was some ether on the wick and quickly used her lighter to light it, turning the wick wheel up and lowering the glass to make the flame larger and the light all the more intense.

Nicola placed the bag down on the nearest lobster pot and took off her beret as Samantha quickly took off her jacket. They placed them, with their trousers and shoes, on the crate next to the bag as they stripped down to their swimming costumes, taking from the bag their swimming shoes and caps.

Samantha watched as Nicola carefully fastened her cap's strap under her chin then checked that her swimming socks were pulled up to just below her knee. She was aware Samantha was watching her and she turned to her, feeling a little self-conscious as Samantha patted her reassuringly on the arm.

From the bag she took out a smaller oilskin bag with two long drawstrings that had a hard object bulging from inside.

'Ready, baby?' she asked as she looped the drawstrings over one arm.

Nervously, Nicola nodded as Samantha turned the hurricane lamp wheel round anti-clockwise until the flame died.

23

The long, luxurious, highly varnished, walnut walls of the corridor gave way to a set of white metal steps and as O'Keefe reached them, O'Hare and O'Brian staggered down the stairs.

'Is that the last?' he asked the pair as he stood to one side.

'Yes,' O'Hare replied though gritted teeth. The weight was beginning to strain his arms. 'We'll stash this lot and then we'll be ready for the off.'

'Good,' O'Keefe replied. 'I'll be starting the engines then.' He turned and headed back down the corridor as O'Hare and O'Brian entered the master bedroom.

*

From the little hut Samantha and Nicola emerged.

Keeping close to the hut, they crossed over to the warehouses and, staying in the shadows, they made their way tentatively down the quayside, away from the Cœur d'Or, to emerge behind some more packing cases by the dock's edge, ten yards or so along from the yacht.

Nicola peered between a gap in the stack, watching the decks of the Cœur d'Or which were lit by the yacht's own embedded lighting over its walkways and from the cabins and corridors below, spilling though the portholes. Samantha, quickly and keeping low, scuttled over to the water's edge and, peering over, she could see that there was a metal ladder leading into the black water.

She turned and waved to Nicola who quickly joined her, and Samantha leading, they descended into the icy water, so cold, that as soon as her feet touched the rippling black water's surface, Samantha could feel them turn to ice even with the shoes and stockings. As she slipped into the water, for a moment, she couldn't breathe, the shock of the cold taking her breath from her, and she instantly began to shiver.

As the water lapped at her chin, she pulled the floating oilskin bag behind her as she glanced up at Nicola keeping a hold on to the ladder. It was far too deep to feel the bottom and, while she waited, her teeth began to chatter as Nicola slipped into the water beside her.

She tightly gripped the ladder rail as Samantha pointed to the yacht. Nicola followed and with the oilskin bag bobbing behind in tow, they swam, both doing the breast stroke, keeping their faces out of the water as, quietly and unobserved, they followed along the harbour quay, towards the Cœur d'Or.

*

O'Keefe opened the large, white steel door and leaving the two locking levers open, he let the bulkhead door swing open behind him as he came over to the two large, green-painted housings of the diesel engines. There was a brass rail between him and the engines, and between them and at his eye level there was a number of brass gauges, which he checked by tapping the glass a couple of times before throwing a switch by each engine and then pressing another button underneath.

Each time, there was a whirring noise. The engines shuddered and then roared into life. As they did so, the gauges jumped from zero to the midpoint and he checked each set of gauges again.

*

Samantha and Nicola had reached the bow of the Cœur d'Or. The water around them was beginning to get a little more choppy as the low droning sound of the engines echoed all around them.

'You hear that!' Samantha exclaimed as she trod water.

'It's the engines.' Nicola answered, almost swallowing some of the salty water as she less successfully tried to tread water too. 'They must be ready to sail.'

Samantha looked carefully along the boat. The Coeur d'Or was facing the opposite way she had been when they visited her during the day, and as Samantha looked along, she could see the rope steps up to the deck, still lowered and on the water's side.

'There, we'll come on their blind side.' She nodded to the rope ladder to Nicola and then silently they both swam over to it. Without stopping for a breath, Samantha reached up and caught the lower wooden rung and pulled herself up, stretching with her other hand to catch the rung two up from the first and with the momentum pulled herself up until her knee was on the first rung.

She paused for a moment to get her breath back and then to check above her that there was no one moving about. The light spilled from the rooms above, lighting the boat up like a Christmas tree, giving her an easy view of the decks and she could see that none of the smugglers were on her side of the boat.

She carefully hauled herself up the next two rungs and then, crouching down, she turned back to Nicola, who was beginning to flag a bit and was tiring fast, more quickly than she had expected. Samantha was already shivering, her body ached with exhaustion and she became concerned as she saw Nicola's face partially sink again into the water before she was able to grab for the lower rung.

Samantha held out her hand, leaning as far as she could down to her while Nicola fought her fatigue to pull herself up onto the first rung. She was slipping, she didn't have the momentum and quickly she stretched out her hand to catch hold of Samantha's. Samantha pulled herself back up the ladder, using her legs and her height like a lever as she clung on tightly to Nicola's wrist. She pulled Nicola up with her and, with a bit of a desperate scramble, Nicola had her feet onto the lower rung.

They took a moment to catch their breath, Samantha checking that the oilskin bag was still by her side. Then, followed by Nicola, Samantha led them up to the main deck.

*

O'Hare and O'Brian replaced the lid on top of the empty crate. O'Hare gathered up his crowbar and O'Brian threw the now light crate up onto his shoulder.

'Put that with the rest in the truck and then put the truck round back. We'll sail in ten minutes,' O'Hare ordered.

'Righty-ho,' O'Brian replied as he headed out of the master bedroom.

*

They reached the top of the ladder and with no one around, they both quickly and quietly rushed over to the side of the lounge, and squatting under its windows, they waited momentarily, listening for any sounds.

Despite the water dripping from them and their costumes clinging to them in the cold night air, neither girl felt cold now. The exhaustion of swimming to the yacht was gone and the fire of the adrenaline coursing through their veins made them feel so very alive. As they carefully sneaked along the deck to the sliding door a few feet from them, a little steam danced off their bare arms.

Samantha gently slid the door open and vigilantly they ventured in.

*

They were coming down the stairs leading to the inner part of the yacht when suddenly they were both gripped by the icy sting of fear as they could hear someone whistling along the corridor. Quickly they raced to the bottom of the stairs and slipped into a room marked 'Stores', just to the left of them. Further down the corridor a door opened as their door closed and, carrying the empty crate, O'Brian appeared, completely unaware that they were there. He slipped the crate off his shoulder and, holding it by one of the rope handles, he then climbed the stairs, still whistling as he went.

It all went quiet once more. The stores door opened slightly and Samantha and Nicola, one head over the other, looked out in opposite directions and then facing the alternate direction, before looking at each other with a sense of relief stretched across their faces. 'Come on,' Samantha encouraged Nicola.

Quietly slipping out of the store room, they began to make their way along the corridor when they heard a door opening and quickly they dashed back up the corridor and back into the store room just as   O'Hare appeared and started to head towards the stairs.

O'Hare paused and at first looked up to the upper level, as he had a troubling thought in the back of his mind that he'd forgotten something. Then, as it came to him, he headed around the stairs to another set of stairs behind them that went down to the next level. Leaning over the rail he shouted down.

'We ready down there?'

O'Keefe emerged holding his ringing ears.

'She's running to speed,' O'Keefe replied. 'You can cast off whenever.'

'Good. We'll just wait for O'Brian to get back.'

O'Keefe joined him and the two men then climbed the stairs to the upper level.

Everything was quiet again as Samantha and Nicola emerged from the store room. Gingerly they headed down the corridor and reached the first main bedroom. Without a word, Samantha pointed to the door. Nicola nodded and they both entered.

Samantha closed the door gently then turned the lock. It snapped shut with a crisp click.

*

The master bedroom was the most opulent room on the ship. Its white ivory coloured wooden panels, each carved with a naval-themed decoration and set inside the walnut beading making a larger wall panel, created a predominantly clean, crisp, white panorama all around the room, giving a brilliant, spacious airy feel to it, more palatial than most of the hotels Samantha had ever stayed in. The bed and the door were walnut and the bedside tables which were walnut with ivory coloured beading inlaid, only the peach carpet and bedspread and matching lampshades created any contrast in colour as even the white clam wall shades were etched to look like ivory.

The walls and wardrobes were all ivory panels.

Samantha knew all the staterooms were the same, but on a smaller scale and only had ivory panels in the doors. For a moment, she felt a sudden overwhelming feeling of despair and disdain for herself and anyone wealthy who could have owned such a yacht, as for the first time, seeing it as she saw it now, it occurred to her just how many working class men and women, whose families were living in small, overcrowded terrace houses, the crumbling slums in the shadow of the large black smoke belching factories all up and down the country, six to eight of them to a living room smaller than this one single bedroom, desperately trying to eke out a meagre existence when one person could afford something as opulent as this yacht, which to him, would have been little more than a diversion, a toy to enjoy once or twice a year.

Just one square foot of ivory panel on this boat, to have been carved, carefully painted and fitted, would have cost the owner as much as a dockworker's monthly wage, provided he was able to secure enough working days to fill a month. Having seen those people dressed in shabby old clothes, struggling to survive, yet working so hard just to earn an early grave, the thought of both those things sickened her to the very pit of her soul.

Things would have to change.

Normally she took her wealth for granted. Normally the flaunting of such wealth did very little to impress her, largely because it was so commonplace in her society. Everyone had expensive furniture, paintings, sculptures and could spend a hundred pounds or more on a night's entertainment so that none of it had any value.

Even a boat like this, just days before, hadn't seemed exceptional. If it had belong to Porky or any of her other London-set friends, she'd probably not even noticed the ivory or the walnut finish or how all the woodwork was French polished. She would have never noticed the hours of craftsmen's labour, wasted on those too blind to care and who were in little more than an arms race to show off just how much they could spend to make those others they called their friends feel inferior.

But this had been Pierre's boat, someone wealthy, yet not someone she would have associated with flaunting his wealth like Porky to impress in a crowd, as he was a self-made man, made so by his talents as a racing driver. Now, she realised how absurd the conspicuous consumption of wealth was and how childish it all was. Maybe because of the heightened anxiety, who knew, but now she was appalled.

Then Samantha's mind returned to the smugglers and for a moment she felt sorry for them. If it was drink and tobacco they were bringing in, or shipping around the country to avoid the tax, in these hard times, who could blame them, and for a moment, her loyalty to the law or to the poor was torn.

Still dripping onto the expensive carpet, Nicola watched as Samantha opened her oilskin bag and took out a small cake tin. She peered under the bed as Samantha placed the tin on the nightstand and with a little effort, opened it to reveal her camera wrapped up in a scarf to stop it moving.

She took the lens cap off and checked the film was rolled on ready. Then, as Nicola checked a cupboard on the other side of the cabin, she opened the nearest wardrobe.

Seeing nothing other than the clothes rails and the drawers, Samantha was bemused as she closed the door and, turning to Nicola, she sighed.

'I'm sure that that bimbo with the box must have come out of here.'

'Ab-so-lute-ly,' Nicola agreed.

'And so, whatever they're smuggling must be in here too?' Nicola nodded. 'So where is it?' Samantha asked rhetorically.

'Some of the big old houses up our way have these hidden rooms in the wall. They're called priest's holes,'

Nicola replied, helpfully adding, 'to hide priests in.'

'Oh, I say, how novel!' Samantha exclaimed as Nicola continued.

'I think it was during the reign of Queen Elizabeth.'

'So you think they might be smuggling priests?' Samantha asked.

'They sounded Irish to me,' Nicola replied.

'And how,' Samantha agreed. 'So why would they be trying to smuggle priests. It's not like they're short of a few out there? Anyway, you couldn't get a priest in one of those boxes, so what else could it be?'

Nicola began to look around the room. Feeling the relief on one of the wall panels, she replied, 'Don't know. But if the principle used back home was applied to what they're smuggling, maybe there's a secret panel in this room?'

'Atta girl!' Samantha grinned. At times Nicola was just like the bright cinder to her damp logs. 'I'm such a Dumb Dora. You're right. Let's look, shall we?'

They both carefully started to examine the wall panels, feeling the carved reliefs, pushing at the panels, when suddenly there was a loud click and, as Nicola stepped back, the wall panel in front of her hinged forward and swung open to reveal a number of rifles racked up and tied together against the wall.

'Horsefeathers!' Samantha swore. 'They're wise guys?'

'You mean…' Nicola shivered nervously as she glanced back to the door, 'they're gunrunners?'

'Ab-so-lute-ly, baby.' Samantha nodded and, stepping back, she adjusted her lens and prepared to take a picture.

'The beasts!!' Nicola swore.

'We can't let them cross the Irish Sea with their weapons.' Samantha took a picture and quickly rolled on her film. 'If these get into the hands of these wise guys, then the lives of many men, women and children could be lost. It was one thing when they were fighting just the army and the Black and Tans but now!' She took another picture.

'But you heard them,' Nicola reminded her. 'They're going to sail in ten minutes.'

'Then we're going to have to do as we originally planned to.' Samantha smiled. 'Move her ourselves!'

'When she was out in the harbour, that seemed easy. When we thought there wasn't going to be anyone about, that all I was going to have to do was keep a watch and you were going to find the evidence, take a picture of it and then hand it to the police, it was simple,' Nicola spoke with a little nervous tremor in her voice. 'But now, and with these wise guys on board, it's not going to be so easy!'

'I grant you, they're a little hardboiled,' Samantha admitted as Nicola sighed nervously. 'But we stick to the plan, but also head out of the harbour,' Samantha reassured her, giving her a little encouraging hug. 'Hopefully Albert will be back before they can take back control.'

Nicola thought for a moment. As plans went, it wasn't much, but then, they'd come too far now to just walk away.

'Then we must take steps to protect ourselves and prevent those bimbos from taking us, against our will!' Nicola replied.

Samantha grinned adding, 'I think we can. You with me baby?'

Nicola nodded and they hugged each other for support.

24

Samantha stood by the open door to the master bedroom, the oilskin bag hanging at her side, its drawstrings looped over her head and shoulder. Nicola came to stand next to her and together they glanced along the corridor, checking no one was coming the other way. Silently Samantha closed the door and quickly they headed over to the stairs that led down to the engine room.

Samantha led the way as they rushed down the steps and along the short corridor to the bulkhead door into the engine room and, as Nicola stood outside looking back to the stairs, Samantha peered in. The room was empty and, after she tapped Nicola gently on the shoulder, they both went in.

The room was filled with a heavy, heady humming noise as they swiftly raced over to the two pounding engines. When they reached them, Samantha took a gentle hold of Nicola's shoulder.

'Wait,' she told her as she began to think her idea through. 'If we do move her now, they'll just come in here and shut her down before we've got out of the harbour. Maybe we should shut down the engines and remove the compressors.'

Nicola glanced around the room. At the far end of the room she noticed a set of steps leading out of the engine room.

'Why?' she asked.

'Because without the compressor,' Samantha replied, 'the engines can't pump the air-diesel mix that fires in the cylinder heads.'

'No, why bother?' Nicola continued. 'Look, you see those stairs. They lead up to the bridge. If you remember, we came down them first when the Harbour Master showed us the bridge. There's a short corridor to the galley and stateroom, but it's an independent corridor. If we lock off the cross hatches and the one in here, then no one will be able to enter the engine room that way and or come up behind us on to the bridge. These doors are watertight and, once they're shut, if we can lock them off, they'd need an acetylene welding torch or dynamite to get them open.'

Samantha turned back to the bulkhead door thinking it might just work. She turned back to Nicola and kissed her softly on the lips.

'Atta girl! You're so clever.'

Nicola smiled broadly as the pride began to well up inside her. Samantha turned back to the door and, as she crossed to it, she added, 'We need to lock this door.' But as she looked at it more closely, she could see that there were no bolts. 'Horsefeathers!' she swore as she turned back to the engine room. She needed something to hold the door in place. Her eyes scanned the room, when suddenly she saw it, a large spanner hanging on a cord by the side of the nearest engine.

'Quick, pass me that large spanner.' She pointed to it.

Nicola grabbed it off the hook and rushed over to Samantha, who was studying the back of the door.

'There you go.'

Samantha took the spanner from her.

'I'll need a box of some kind too.'

Nicola nodded and glanced around, looking along the floor, when she saw an oil can and, as Samantha closed the bulkhead door and pushed the levers up so that the door was shut, Nicola collected the can.

'Thank you.' Samantha took the can and placed it up against the door. Then, having placed the spanner with its jaws against the lower lever, she wedged the long handle into the top of the can. She tried to lower the upper bulkhead levers but the lower lever wouldn't move and, as they worked as one, no matter how much she tried, they wouldn't budge.

'As good as locked.' She slapped her hands in a single clap.

'One of us will need to slip off the mooring ropes!' Nicola exclaimed, pointing to the outside of the ship.

'I'll do that,' Samantha assured her. 'You concentrate on keeping her steady, baby.'

Nicola nodded.

'All we need now is something to block the other two doors just the same.'

'There's a fire axe and another spanner and lots of cans,' Nicola replied, pointing a thumb over her shoulder.

'Atta girl.' Samantha grinned.

Nicola felt a bit nervous, but she smiled to reassure Samantha as they collected up what they needed and both made their way over to the far set of steps.

*

The bridge was empty as Samantha and Nicola entered. Looking out of the windows to the quayside, they could see O'Brian walking back from behind a hut and they watched as he reached the gangplank.

When he was out of sight, Nicola slid the bridge door open and gingerly made her way to the side rail and peered over. She could see the shadows of three to five men. It was hard to gauge how many as they were moving around in the cocktail lounge. She heard the door close, cutting off some of the light as O'Brian entered. She waited a couple of seconds but all the sounds she could hear were coming from inside the lounge. A glance along the deck showed it was clear and she headed back into the bridge as Samantha joined her.

'There's one rope at the front and one at the back. Judging by the lights, they all seem to be in the cocktail lounge,' Nicola told Samantha helpfully as she looked along the length of the yacht.

'Should make things easier,' Samantha replied. 'You said it was well stocked!'

'Well, now we know why!' Nicola agreed as she slid open the bridge door. 'Good luck.'

Samantha paused and stroked Nicola's arm softly. She wanted to reassure her that nothing was going to happen. Once the boat was moving, they would be safe, but they both knew, as soon as they started, anything could happen. She took her oilskin bag and hung it over one of the voice pipes.

The fear was there in her eyes but they both pretended it wasn't and Samantha slipped away carefully down the steps towards the upper deck.

Nicola entered the bridge, slid the door shut again and watched the quay nervously, keeping her fingers crossed, praying inside that Samantha would be alright.

25

Samantha swiftly made her way down the second flight of steps. As she reached the main deck, she paused for a moment to listen for any irregular sound. Apart from the sound of the harbour bell on the buoy, swaying with the movement of the sea as it rolled into the harbour, and the faint sound of music from within the cocktail lounge, everything seemed fine to her. She could see no movement and, after taking a steadying deep breath, she quickly made her way over to the gangplank, keeping bent low so as not to be seen from the windows of the lounge.

As she reached the gangplank, she looked back to the cocktail lounge. No one was looking out, so she ran down it as fast as she could and onto the quay.

*

O'Hare and his fellow conspirators were all standing in a little knot near the cocktail lounge bar, each holding a glass filled with whisky as the gramophone, on the table next to the piano, played some merry little Irish ditty.

'Well, lads.' He held his glass aloft and the others raised their glasses too. 'Here's to another successful trip.'

*

With all her strength, she lifted the loop off the mooring post then let the bow rope slip from her hands and fall with a dull splash into the water.

She looked up to the yacht decks, but no one had stirred and so she sprinted down to the stern as fast as she could and heaved off that mooring rope too. As it slipped off the quay, Samantha sprinted to the gangplank.

The yacht was already beginning to drift and, as it did so, the gangplank was slowly being dragged off the quayside. When Samantha reached it, she didn't stop. She ran as fast as her burning limbs would carry her, only crouching down on the main deck to pause for breath as the gangplank fell into the water, with a loud echoing splash. She didn't wait. She had little time now and rushed to the stairs, scrambling up them to the bridge.

*

The four men stopped drinking and as they each looked at one another a little bemused, O'Hare rushed to a window on the quayside of the boat.

'The gangplank's gone!' he cried with astonishment as O'Connor rushed over to the other side of the room and looked out the window.

'We're drifting.'

'We can't be!' O'Keefe exclaimed. 'We're moored.'

O'Hare turned back to the room.

'We are. We're drifting from the quay.'

Suddenly the vibration and the sound of the engines powering up reverberated around the cocktail lounge, making the bottles in the cabinet tinkle as they shook.

'Someone's on the bridge!' O'Hare cried.

'Someone's stealing our boat!' O'Connor couldn't believe the audacity of some people.

'Quick, to the bridge.' O'Hare cried leading them to the quayside door as they followed him out.

The four men bounded out onto the lower deck. O'Hare grabbed the mahogany rail opposite and stared out to the quay. The boat was already several feet away from the quay and he heard the bell of the chadburn ring once followed by the sound of the whirling propellers chopping in the water, beginning to echo from over the side as the yacht began to move slowly towards the harbour entrance.

He turned for the stairs, the others following as he raced up, two at a time, hauling himself up the steep incline with the aid of the rails. Just as O'Hare got within a couple of rungs from the top, he looked up as a large object filled his sky, hurtling towards him. He was suddenly struck on the head with an oar wielded by a definitely mean-looking Samantha.

The force of the oar was so strong and so sudden that O'Hare fell backwards, losing his grip on the rails and toppling into O'Connor, who fell backwards with him into O'Brian. He then fell with them both into O'Keefe and they all tumbled in a large heap on the floor.

*

Nicola turned the wheel to her left, passing three of the balusters past her axle as she watched her compass. Then as she turned to the right, she watched for the harbour light to come to the side of the bridge window and, on seeing it, she turned the wheel to the right four times. As it slowed, the Coeur d'Or began to line up with the harbour entrance to leave.

She gripped the two levers on the chadburn, pushed them forward to the end, and then back to the position 'Ahead Slow', the indicator arm stopping over the words as the chadburn's bell rang out the instruction and the yacht automatically obeyed. Her engines shuddered as they began to spin faster at the number of revolutions needed to move the heavy vessel steadily in a progressively slow manner. The yacht began to creep forward as Nicola, turning the wheel both left and right slightly, held the compass setting steady and aimed for the gap in the sea wall.

Her stomach was already churning and she'd wished she'd taken a pill, but with a bit of deep breathing, she began to quell it a little and told herself it was only the fear that was making her feel that way.

The bridge door slid open and in rushed Samantha. Without stopping and without Nicola paying her any attention, she rushed in to the ante-room in the short corridor that led to the steps.

There, under the chart table, she found a long, black, metal box, and slid it out. She tried to lift it but she found it was too heavy for her and so dragged a little towards the entranceway.

The box had a latch over an eye hook, but no lock and quickly she flipped it off, opened the lid and inside were a number of blue rockets with red-coloured nosecones. Attached to the inside of lid was the base, a long brass-like tube with a bi-pod stand and a small tinderbox lighter.

Quickly she scooped up the lighter and slipped it into the thigh band of her swimming costume before pulling the tube and stand out. Then, after taking a couple of rockets out too, she gathered them all up into her arms and carefully made her way back onto the bridge.

Samantha could see the harbour entrance looming large in front of them. A sense of pride filled her heart as she cried, 'Atta girl. You just hold her steady, baby. I'll get us some help.' Then she came over to Nicola and, as Nicola grimaced because the wheel tried to whip itself out of her hands, she turned to her to kiss her softly on the lips.

'Good luck.'

'You too.'

They held hands momentarily to reassure one another. Then, as Nicola went back to concentrating on negotiating the harbour entrance, Samantha swept quickly out from the bridge.

*

O'Hare's head was gashed and was sore, but this didn't concern him. He was angry, not just because he'd allowed his boat to be taken over, but that this was by a couple of women and his pride wouldn't stand for such a humiliation.

He turned to the others, as they too began to recover and pick themselves up, and snarled, 'Darn wildcat flappers!' Then, taking the revolver out of his jacket, he waved his men on and they followed him, racing up the stairs once more. Just as O'Hare reached the last couple of rungs from the top, he was struck on the head with an oar as Samantha peered down on him, watching as O'Hare fell backwards.

He squeezed the trigger. There was a loud crack, a flash and wood splintered as the side of the oar's blade was sheared off. O'Hare knocked into O'Connor, who fell backwards with him into O'Brian, the three of them crashing into O'Keefe, and they all collapsed once more into a large heap on the floor.

Samantha laid the oar by the steps and gathered together quickly the rockets and launcher. Then, without a pause for breath, she ran past the bridge and the lifeboat and carried on to the back of the boat, just past the funnel, and placed the launcher on the side by the rail, pointing out to sea.

She placed the rockets down and set up the bi-pod stand, clipping it into the launcher tube making a sturdy tripod. Then, picking up one of the rockets, she inserted it into the tube, taking care to push the fuse cord, the long twist of paper, out though the hole in the side at the launcher's base.

She quickly slipped the tinderbox from her swimsuit and opened it, taking out the striking iron. Holding it close to the twist of paper, she struck the iron twice. There was a spark and it caught with a small bright flame as the powder inside the twist burnt ferociously. She stood back quickly as the rocket began to smoke.

*

O'Hare and his men looked up and watched as the rocket shot up with a sudden fizz into the sky, to explode only moments later leaving a large, red, burning fireball hovering up above them, illuminating everything under its fiery glow.

'Dammed flappers! They'll bring the whole of Devon down on us!' O'Hare seethed, flexing the grip of his fists a couple of times as if, in his mind, he was crushing their necks with his hands.

'They'll bring the law down upon us, they will!' O'Connor was panicking, but O'Hare was beginning to calm himself down. He had to act fast and he knew it. O'Connor was right. Time was now against them and he had to take back control of his yacht.

'O'Keefe, go and turn the engines off!' he barked.

'Right,' O'Keefe replied as he turned and headed quickly back into the cocktail lounge.

'That's all well and fine,' O'Connor wittered on, his nerves beginning to fray, 'but what about those flappers? If we don't set sail within the next half an hour, it will be daylight when we reach Ireland!'

'I know!' O'Hare shouted at him angrily, slapping him around the head. 'Then we're going to have to take the bridge.' He picked his gun up off the deck. 'You with me, lads?'

Just then there was another whoosh and, as they spun round, they could see another rocket explode high up in the sky.

26

Samantha left the launcher, turned and ran with all her might past the lifeboat and bridge, grabbing the oar. As she peered over the rail down the stairs, there was a bright, white flash and the familiar crack of a gunshot that echoed around the metal sides of the stairs. She ducked back for cover and noticed in the oar, just inches from her face, there was a neat, round bullet hole.

Carrying the oar with her, she ran back to the bridge.

*

Nicola was still holding them on a steady course, turning the wheel to the right so that the boat turned left to come on a parallel course to the coast as they came through the harbour wall and rounded the small lighthouse on the arm jutting out into the sea. Samantha closed and locked the bridge door behind her.

'I just hope someone sees those rockets!' Samantha exclaimed more in hope than in expectation.

*

He'd reached the door to the engine room but as he tried to open it, O'Keefe was surprised to find that the door lever wouldn't budge. He pulled with both hands, tried to shake it up and down and then lift it like he was lifting a set of barbells, but it wouldn't give.

His arms ached and his hands burnt with pain, but for all his might he couldn't open the door. He swore and kicked at it with frustration so hard that he hurt his foot. Reluctantly he turned and hobbled back up the stairs.

*

O'Hare and his other two men tentatively crept their way up the stairs, his gun ready and pointing from his hip up to the upper deck, as he waited with bated breath for another swipe from Samantha's oar. But this time it didn't come and, reaching the upper deck, he could see Nicola at the wheel and, as O'Connor and O'Brian joined him, he levelled his gun to take aim.

*

Suddenly the boat rolled slightly, caught by the bigger waves of the sea, and Nicola struggled to hold the wheel steady. O'Hare fired, and the window in front of her exploded. She ducked for cover and O'Hare, O'Connor and O'Brian rushed for the bridge door.

O'Hare pulled at it, but the latch slipped from his hand and he cursed the locked door. He took aim at the door handle and then fired twice into it. The metal sparked and the wooden frame splintered. He pulled hard at the door and it slid open.

O'Hare burst in. He suddenly felt a pain and fell sideways as he was clouted on the side of the head by the swinging, glancing swipe of Samantha's oar. He staggered to one side, dropping his gun and, continuing to stagger, almost fell to the floor as his legs turned to jelly. O'Connor rushed in and, as O'Hare sank to the floor, O'Connor grabbed for the oar. Samantha flicked it below his grasp, as if she was wielding a quarterstaff and then swung it out wide of his grip, before reversing it in her hands, and with the narrow pointed end, pushing him back into the path of O'Brian, forcing them both back out off the bridge.

Head spinning, O'Hare began to recover. It felt as if he had downed two whole bottles of whisky the night before and then gone seven rounds with the Moy Tír Na nÓg Gaelic football team. As he began to pick himself up, rubbing his head, Nicola watched him out of the corner of her eye.

'Sam!' she shouted and Samantha swung round from the bridge door, still poking the pointed end of the oar at the other two. Seeing O'Hare getting up, she swung the oar at him and clobbered him square on the side of the head, so that he fell dazed to the floor again.

O'Keefe arrived at the top of the stairs and quickly he joined O'Brian and O'Connor on the deck in front of the bridge.

'Somehow they've locked the engine room. Our only way down's through the bridge,' he gasped trying to get his breath back.

'Then we have to get on the bridge,' O'Brian emphasised to them, tapping his bare wrist as if he was wearing a watch to indicate time was running out.

'Follow me.' O'Connor cried taking control and together all three of them assaulted the bridge in a last forlorn charge.

*

O'Hare groaned as he started to crawl on all fours, only for the oar to come crashing down on the back of his head. There was a loud shout and Samantha turned around to see O'Connor with O'Brian and O'Keefe just behind him rushing onto the bridge. She turned levelling the oar like she was trying to dam the tide, but O'Brian picked up the gun and pointed it directly at her. Suddenly there was an overwhelming sense that it was all over. Her bravery faded as she became gripped with fear and let the oar drop from her hands.

The three men grinned gleefully at the two women, as Samantha, her hands raised, stepped slowly backwards until she was standing by Nicola's side.

O'Brian slowly pulled back on the gun's hammer, it clicked as it locked in place and with a calm, steady hand, he pointed it right at Samantha's heart. He grinned, his finger closing tighter around the trigger. She tensed, her eyes almost closed as she waited for the sudden crack, when suddenly the whole yacht was bathed in a bright, harsh, white light.

Drifting over the night air, in a slightly echoing voice, they heard 'This is H.M.S Kent, to stricken steam vessel. We're coming alongside.'

'H.M.S Kent! She's that new County-class cruiser, with a top speed of 31.5 knots!' O'Brian cried looking at his comrades, but they could offer no hope, as they nervously waited for the Royal Navy warship to come alongside.

*

The Cœur d'Or was dwarfed next the heavy cruiser. With her four huge gun turrets, and a seagoing biplane resting behind the last of three funnels, she was 632 feet 9 inches long, 66 feet wide and 13,315 tons of pure menace. Just one of her torpedoes alone would have turned the Cœur d'Or to little more than matchwood. A small launch was lowered over the side and made its way over to the Cœur d'Or, before the heavily armed boarding party clambered up the side rope ladder and onto the lower deck.

*

Nicola and Samantha stood in the middle of the bridge with a ring of six burly sailors standing with the backs to them, each man rigidly to attention.

Captain Carmichael, a tall handsome man in his mid-forties, resplendent in his long greatcoat, looked along the corridor and over to the stairs from the lower deck as he watched the young Lieutenant Selkirk, dressed in a greatcoat but with less golden piping around the cuffs and carrying two plain greatcoats, reached the top step and headed on to the bridge.

'Well done, Lieutenant. Quickly hand them to the girls.'

Lieutenant Selkirk saluted his captain.

'Sir.' He then crossed over to the ring of men, handing the coats over the top for Samantha to take.

The Lieutenant joined his Captain as Nicola and Samantha quickly slipped the coats on, the very heavy, warming woollen coats felt good against their shivering wet bodies as their little trembling fingers frantically fastened the large brass buttons. Once they were ready, the circle broke and, as Selkirk and Carmichael then turned to them, Samantha's and Nicola's little squelching footsteps echoed as they crossed to meet them.

'That's better.' Captain Carmichael beamed with satisfaction. 'We can't have two frail little foxes like yourselves running around naked in public, can we now?'

'Quite!' Samantha exclaimed.

'All a bit too continental for my liking,' Captain Carmichael added, bristling slightly as the very thought of such loose ways appalled him.

'Nice of you to bring us these coats, Captain,' Samantha thanked him. 'They're nice and warm and, what with the water being so cold, my friend and I were beginning to feel a bit of a chill.'

'That's quite alright, Miss,' Captain Carmichael replied with a little friendly salute. 'Glad to be of service.' He glanced over to the sailor at the wheel. 'Helm, take us into the harbour.' Then turning to the other crewmen standing waiting instructions, he barked. 'And would someone rustle us up a couple of hot Bovrils up here sharpish? These young ladies need reviving.'

One of the sailors quickly snapped to attention, turned and exited through the back corridor to go down below as the others left to go about their other duties.

'We're just grateful, Captain, that you came alongside.' Samantha smiled warmly.

'Was a stroke of the most extraordinary luck, Miss,' Captain Carmichael continued. 'We'd heard that there might be some greasy Spanish fishing boats in the area stealing our pilchards and we were given orders by the First Lord of the Admiralty, the Right Honourable William Bridgeman MP, to blast these nasty dagos out the water. Having just finished our sea trials we were hoping for a bit of action, but then we had this most extraordinary Morse code message come through, from the Devon Coast Guard, saying that there were some Irish gun runners trying to smuggle some weapons into the Free State in our patrol area and to be on the lookout. Then when we saw your flares, well.' He shrugged. 'We knew that we had to answer a distress call, but not for one moment we never imagined that you might have the Irish gun runners on board. It was just sheer luck I already had my men armed and ready in case we ran into those blasted dagos.' He paused to sigh wistfully, as he added, 'I know it's not as much fun as sinking fishing boats but all the same, Miss, I think it's been a jolly good night all round.'

'Well, if you need any photos, we took some pictures,'

Samantha added helpfully, pointing to her oilskin bag.

'No need to worry about them, Miss. We have the guns themselves. Should be enough to hang them, don't you worry.

The sailor returned with a tray upon which were four mugs of steaming hot Bovril, which he passed first to Nicola and Samantha who took one each to cradle in their icy cold hands before offering one to Captain Carmichael, who took one, and then Lieutenant Selkirk who took the last.

'Ah, Bovril.' Captain Carmichael took a sip. 'Just right as it's almost midnight.'

*

With the sailors on board to crew the yacht, it wasn't long before the Cœur d'Or was safely moored again, though facing the other way round and a new gangplank had been set in place so they could reach the quayside.

On the quay there were a couple of police vans, a couple of police cars and a lot of armed police officers waiting. Parked amidst all this was the shining, polished outline of the Riley, as Albert waited nervously with Detective Inspector Marriot, a tall man with a square, chiselled jaw, deep-set eyes and dark brown hair, which though cut short, still poked out from under his grey trilby, his hands thrust deep into his trench-coat pockets and beside him, his subordinate, Sergeant Finch, a short, granite-looking man with a harsh face and stocky build, who stood watching intensely, wearing a long black coat and with his gloved hands by his side, staring out at the Cœur d'Or from under the brim of his trilby hat.

Marriot and Albert watched as two armed sailors escorted the Irishmen off the boat, handcuffed to each other with the solemn look of defeat ingrained on their faces as they descended the gangplank and into the arms of the waiting police officers, who led them to their waiting vans.

Another sailor escorted Samantha and Nicola down the gangplank, still smothered deep inside their greatcoats and, on seeing where Albert was waiting, they both rushed over to him. Detective Inspector Marriot looked them up and down and sighed to himself, hiding his overriding disapproval.

'Albert, would you collect our bag, please? It's in that hut.' Samantha nodded to it. 'Over there.'

'Miss.' He nodded and headed over to the hut as Detective Inspector Marriot stepped forward.

'Congratulations, Miss Bishop.' He nodded to Samantha and turned to Nicola. 'Miss White.' He continued in a very official manner. 'Sergeant Finch and I raced down on the night train as soon as we received your telegram.' Sergeant Finch nodded to them both, touching the tip of his trilby with his index finger as they politely smiled back. 'Had to make them hold it for a full five minutes, but I'm glad we did.'

'I'm just glad you made it in time, Inspector,' Samantha replied.

'Yes, quite,' Nicola echoed, her teeth chattering in the cold night air.

'I must just say,' Marriot continued in his dry, well-rehearsed style, 'that was most splendid work. We've been after these scoundrels for a while. We knew that there was an Irish cell smuggling weapons into the Free State, to use against W. T. Cosgrave's Cumann na nGaedheal government and I must thank you both for filling in the blanks. We had no idea just how many of them there were, where they were operating from, what weapons they were smuggling, or how they were moving the money. We didn't know who their middleman was or how they were actually shipping the guns over to Ireland. But now we know the details. O'Hare and his gang are going to be spending a long time behind bars.'

'We were just glad to help.' Samantha shrugged. 'We

were just worried these bimbos might be trying to make out our friend Sylvie as being all wet, because she's just a tomato, not a wise guy like them and we thought that they might be staging some kind of double-cross. I'm mean, on the level, I'm not one to take any wooden nickels and I hate to see my friends taken for saps. We had no idea we were taking a ride with a gang of torpedoes, but you're here now, Inspector, so that's swell.'

'Quite,' he replied, oblivious to what she'd said, before continuing, 'Of course we can't officially announce publicly that a couple of young, delicate waifs like yourselves have helped in preventing an international arms ring from operating from within British territorial waters. It's not really the done thing. The public wouldn't be prepared for such a shock.'

'Ab-so-lute-ly!' Samantha sympathised.

'But my commissioner says, as a token of our appreciation, he would like me to give you...' Marriot searched deeply into his coat pocket and took out a couple of small brown envelopes. 'These coupons for a whole pound each to spend on make-up, that sort of thing.' He handed one of the envelopes to Samantha. 'What with you both being a couple of modern young ladies and all, he thought that would make up for not having any public recognition.'

Samantha took the envelope with a forced, warm smile that she was sure was going to crack her icy cold cheeks.

'That's fine, Detective Inspector,' she replied.

He then handed the other envelope to Nicola and, as she took it, not really sure what to do next, Detective Inspector Marriot gave them both a small salute, spun around on his heels and then strode quickly away to a waiting police car, with Sergeant Finch in tow, as Samantha and Nicola looked disappointedly at their envelopes.

Albert crossed over to the Riley, placed the bag in the

boot and, as he opened the back door, Samantha and Nicola quickly clambered in. He closed their door and, as they wriggled under the travel rug, he climbed into the driver's seat. Closing the door, he turned to them, as Samantha slipped the oilskin bag out from under her greatcoat and placed it carefully into the door pocket before picking up her handbag. As she took her cigarette case out and opened it, he asked, 'What would you like to do now, Miss?'

Samantha turned to Nicola, who was still shivering slightly, then took out a cigarette and snapped the case shut. 'I think back to the cottage. Then I think you should book us into the Grand tomorrow. Let's have one night of luxury and get ourselves acclimatised back into civilisation before we head on back to London.'

'Right you are, Miss.'

'I think I've had enough of the sea and seamen.' Samantha sighed as she looked at her envelope again. Turning back to glance over to the yacht once more, she quipped, 'I'll be glad to never see the Cœur again!'

She lit her cigarette as Nicola snuggled up beside her. Albert started the engine. It shuddered into life and, after a moment to select the gear, the little Riley gently pulled away, its headlights illuminating the harbour road as they headed back to town.

*

There was a large fire burning halfway up the hill, and as they came along the narrow road, the fire became brighter and higher over the hedgerows.

*

'Looks like someone's burning the stubble,' Samantha remarked half asleep as she snuggled closer to Nicola who was quietly sleeping with her head resting on Samantha's shoulder.

'Bit early for that,' Albert remarked. 'They haven't even harvested any crops yet!'

She sat a little more upright and looked out over to the orange haze in the near distance.

'You know, you're right, Albert. This is most queer. You don't think it's some strange custom they have in these parts, like burning a huge effigy to bring about a successful harvest.'

'Again, Miss, be a bit late for that!'

'Ab-so-lute-ly,' she agreed, puzzled by it all, but, too tired to really care, she snuggled back down under the travel rug and cuddled up next to Nicola.

*

They turned into the cottage grounds. The Riley shuddered to a stop, the three of them sitting there, as in front of them the entire cottage was ablaze.

*

Samantha leant forward, she was in complete shock.

'Horsefeathers!' she turned to Albert. 'What's happened?' Then she slapped the back of his seat.

'All your nice clothes, Miss.' He sighed.

'And yours too, Albert. When we get back to London, I'll replace them immediately, don't you worry.'

'Thank you, Miss.' He turned to her and with a slight smile asked, 'To the Grand now, Miss?'

'If you would, Albert,' she replied, sitting back with Nicola, putting an arm around her as they slipped back under the travel rug.

'At least there's nothing to pack.' He shrugged and then put the car into reverse.

'No,' she agreed. 'Though we will need to go into town tomorrow and pick up some underwear, we can't go back in just trousers and jacket. Why, we haven't even got a blouse between us!'

27

Albert was standing at the sink, drying a cup. On the table there were the usual breakfast things laid out on a tray ready and a larger teapot standing next to it, ready to filled with hot water, as the kettle gently hissed on the lighted stove.

Just then the doorbell rang. The indicator box over the hallway door dropped its marker over the square under the words 'front door' and so he placed the cup down on the table next to the tray, put on his butler's coat and pulled the lever under the box to re-set it before heading at his normal, sedate pace along the corridor to the front door.

The doorbell rang again and, as he reached the front door, he paused for a moment to ensure his jacket and shirt cuffs were correct before opening it to reveal a young telegram boy standing in front of him in his smart, grey uniform and hat with the red piping.

'Telegram for a Miss Bishop and a Miss White. Is that right? You got two Misses here?'

Albert took the telegram from him and gave him a farthing.

'None of your business,' he replied, shutting the door quickly on the telegram boy before heading back down the corridor to the kitchen with the telegram still in his hand.

*

Samantha and Nicola were both asleep in bed, spooning together, Nicola's arm draped over Samantha's at the waist and, though the sun was shining brightly, the curtains were still drawn shut.

The room itself was a large rectangle, running from the one large centre window that looked out onto the mews.

The room was dominated by the double bed, the head end against the wall opposite the window and near to the door, with the headboard, footboard and springs all painted in a dark biscuit brown, without any inlays or decoration added, though around the top of the panels, both on the headboard and the footboard there were two parallel lines, moulded to follow the curve from one post to the other. There was an orange spread covering the blankets and both the sheets were a shiny pink satin. Either side of the bed there were two bedside tables, both by the head end and on both there was a tall, slim, chrome pedestal lamp with a wide, red shade, each with a brown, barley-twist cord that disappeared down the back of the table.

As Albert entered carrying the tray on which was the telegram along with their breakfast things, he came round the bed to the far bedside table, passing around the round-shaped orange and brown armchair that faced the bed at its foot, separated by the small, red rug that added a bright splash of colour on the tan carpet that otherwise covered every inch of the bedroom floor.

Behind him there were two paintings, one of a ballerina waiting in the wings of a stage waiting to go on, and another of a ballerina warming up, doing her stretches, as another in the background checked that her pumps were tied up properly. The pictures were hung either side of a large Armoires-style wardrobe. Beside that, just to the side of the wardrobe door on the window side, there was a small chocolate-coloured clothes horse.

He crossed over to the golden tan curtains that hung behind the dressing table with its three-part fantail mirror. Scattered on its surface was an assortment of silver-topped glass bottles, jars and atomisers, as well as a silver and mother-of-pearl backed hairbrush and a small matching hand mirror, Kleenex box and the great assortment of brushes and lipsticks any modern girl could need.

The picture rails, window frames and skirting boards were all the same brown as the bed and though there was a large disc-up shaded lamp in the middle of the cream ceiling, there were at regular intervals around the tan walls a number of white clamshell uplighters, none of which were lit. All the wall and ceiling lights were controlled by just two brass switches on a brass plate just inside the door.

On the other long wall, there were another two paintings, one of a ballerina on the stage, with the spotlight partially silhouetting her as she balanced herself on pointed toes, with one leg raised parallel to the stage. The other was much the same, but the pose was different as if she was about to do a spin.

There was also, at an angle to the dressing table and the armchair, making a loose triangle, a full-length, free-standing mirror.

Above the headboard there was another painting of a ballerina taking her bow on the stage, flowers strewn around her as if they had been thrown by her admiring audience, while she relished their applause.

He slid both curtains back and used the rope tie to hold them open, peering out to the street below as both Samantha and Nicola begin to stir.

'Your tea, Miss. Miss. Oh, and there's a telegram addressed to you both,' he informed them as Samantha began to sit up.

'A telegram.' She wiped the sleep from her eyes. 'I wonder who that can be from?'

'I have no idea, Miss.' He shrugged. 'I didn't take the liberty of finding out.'

'That's alright, Albert.'

'I gave the boy a farthing, Miss.'

'Then help yourself to a farthing from my purse, Albert.'

'Very good, Miss.' He thanked her. 'Shall I pour?' he asked as Nicola began to sit up.

'No, we can manage, Albert,' Samantha replied.

He bowed slightly and they watched as he left.

Nicola passed the telegram to Samantha, who started to open it as Nicola poured them both their teas. She carefully handed a cup and saucer to Samantha, before picking up her own. Samantha placed the telegram on her lap and, after taking a small refreshing sip, she began to read the yellow piece of paper before her.

'It's from Sylvie.' She smiled and took another sip of her tea.

'Yes?' Nicola asked, intrigued to know what it said.

'She says that her crew have arrived safely with the Cœur and have berthed her nicely down there in Cannes.'

'Is that all?' Nicola asked, sipping her tea.

'No.' Samantha read the rest quickly then continued. 'She says she's already found a buyer. Some guy who's doing business in Morocco needs a boat for some exotic product he's looking to export and thinks the Cœur's the perfect vessel for the job!'

'Does she say how much he's offering to pay her for

it?'

'No, but she says the boat's been priced at $100,000 US, so what's that in real money?' Quickly Samantha did the conversion in her head. '£25000 less her mooring fees, which were only £1,7s,3d. She should be a woman of means again.'

'Oh, I am pleased.' Nicola smiled warmly, genuinely happy for Sylvie's good fortune.

'So am I.'

They both sipped their tea as, echoing down the corridor, they could hear the sound of the telephone ringing.

'I think there's a new Ronald Coleman film at the flicks,' Nicola continued. 'Or we could see that one with Clara Bow in 'Wings'. It's a war film, but I doubt she's actually one of those flyboys.'

The phone stopped ringing.

'Yes, be nice to see a flick today,' Samantha agreed. 'I'll have Albert wash down the Alvis before we go.'

They sipped their tea before looking deeply into each other's eyes. After all, there was no rush. The cinema didn't open until two. Samantha put her cup back on the tray and, after taking Nicola's from her and placing it on the tray, she turned to her.

Gently she took Nicola into her arms, caressing her soft body as they moved closer to one another, so close Samantha could feel her heart beating quickly through the thin cotton of her nightdress, her hot sweet breath tantalisingly tickling her wet lips as they parted slightly. Samantha moved her head gently to her right and was just about to kiss Nicola when there was a knock at the door and, as they quickly edged themselves apart, it opened and Albert entered.

'Sorry to disturb you, Miss, but Miss Davenport is on the telephone. Wants to know if you're free this weekend?'

'Provided she doesn't want to go sailing, then yes, I suppose we are.' Samantha shrugged, handing Nicola back her tea. Then, as she picked up her own, Albert with a nod replied, 'Very good, Miss. I'll inform Miss Davenport you will be free.'

He closed the door behind him as he left.

Samantha grinned wickedly.

'Now, where were we?'

THE END

ABOUT THE AUTHOR

Anthony Day was born in Margate, Kent and now lives in Whitstable writing contemporary, science fiction, fantasy and historically based fiction.

OTHER BOOKS BY THIS AUTHOR INCLUDE

MUNCH
THE SIGNAL
WAITING FOR A TRAIN
CALICO JACK OF THE BLACK FLAG: vol 1
CALICO JACK OF THE BLACK FLAG: vol 2
MY FRIEND STEWART